D1219552

THIS SIDE OF THE RIVER

Jeffrey Stayton

The Nautilus Publishing Company

OXFORD, MISSISSIPPI

For information contact Nautilus Publishing, 426 South Lamar Blvd., Suite 16, Oxford, MS 38655.

This is a work of fiction. All names, characters, places and incidents are products of the author's imagination.

ISBN: 978-1-936-946-38-9

The Nautilus Publishing Company
426 South Lamar Blvd., Suite 16
Oxford, Mississippi 38655
Tel: 662-513-0159
www.nautiluspublishing.com
www.JeffreyStayton.com

First Edition

Front cover design by Le'Herman Payton. Front cover photo by Robert Jordan
Title design by Connor Covert

Library of Congress Cataloging-in-Publication Data has been applied for.

10   9   8   7   6   5   4   3   2   1

In memory of my father William S. Stayton
Matt and Jeff miss you, Dad.

AUTHOR'S NOTE

Prior to the twentieth century, soldiers suffering from Post-Traumatic Stress Disorder, or shellshock, were said to be suffering from "nostalgia" or "soldier's heart."

J.S.

Stories are medicine.

          ---Clarissa Pinkola Estes, *Women Who Run With the Wolves*

Myth is the wound we leave
In the time we have—

          ---Eavon Boland, "The Making of an Irish Goddess"

METTA DAHLGREN

W<small>E CHOSE HIM</small>. We needed a champion in the plague year 1865 and since all the good Georgia men were either too dead or shattered beyond recognition, we chose a Texas Ranger no older than myself to lead us north to Ohio—to burn that blackguard Sherman's home to ashes. We had just won the Battle of Savannah and proved that ladies can fire guns just as surely as men can. We had saved our captain from certain hanging and freed his lieutenants to boot. And do you think he promised us Sherman's head on a pike? No, not exactly. Instead, Capt. Harvey produced a ledger with the names and hometowns of some band of Yankees called Northrop's Scouts. He gave his first order then: we would ride north to Yankeedom, find those scouts, burn their homes and kill them all.

"But what about Sherman?" one of our widows, Elisha, demanded.

Our captain, already looking faraway in the eyes, told us, "We savor him for last."

I was always raised to believe that one does not forget that she is a Baldwin, though I must now and forever regard myself as the Widow Dahlgren. And a Baldwin mustn't quibble with her captain once she has freely chosen him. I am still a lady. The war has made partisans of us all, but my girls still ride side-saddle into battle, and I must set the example. We may be armed with Enfield rifles, Colt revolvers and meat cleavers, but my Swainsboro girls are a clean set. We are as well-groomed as our war ponies, I am proud to say. All thirty-three of them are the best riders in my estimation, too. We shall all make excellent scouts. So I did not quibble with my captain then. I mounted Princess Ann and rode north on the march.

Texicans don't walk ten feet if they can ride their horses, and this I found true of our captain. He sat his horse, Snaps, in the most natural way. I am not ashamed to say I find this remarkably attractive in the man. He reminds me of Mr. Dahlgren. Oh, ours was not a lovematch but rather a marriage of persuasion. I had many admirers from the time I developed, but Father dismissed them outright for Mr. Dahlgren, a man twice my age and painfully ugly. I cried on my wedding night. I was inconsolable. It was not until I saw Mr. Dahlgren mount his favorite horse, Jupiter, that I began to see the inner man emerge. I cannot say I loved him then. It wasn't till Mr. Dahlgren fell with Jeb Stuart at Yellow Tavern that I believe I loved the man. How strange to fall so deeply in love with a ghost.

Before the War, when Mr. Dahlgren had insisted I learn how to shoot, I threw a horrendous fit. But he put his foot down. He said, "Mama knew how to shoot and so will you." I hated everything about guns. The noise, the kick, the smoke. I screamed and dropped the revolver the first time I fired it. And Mr. Dahlgren had the temerity to laugh at me! I stormed off. But he resumed the lesson the very next day and every day afterward. I never thought I would need use of such weapons. "That's what I have you for," I told him.

Then Mr. Dahlgren died and Sherman trampled through my everything. Dahlgren House, reduced to smoking Sherman Sentinels. I had forgotten all of my gun lessons, I was so scared. I acted like a complete and utter... lady.

I heard that there was a Texican still fighting Yankees, even after the last army had surrendered. He had even attempted to rescue President Davis from capture. Well, I knew that I had to make adjustments. I was no longer a mere Baldwin. I was now the Widow Dahlgren. I dressed once more in my widow's weeds, holstered my Navy Colt revolvers, sheathed my meat cleaver into my belt, and slung Mr. Dahlgren's Enfield rifle over my shoulder and then mounted Princess Ann to round up all the young widows of Swainsboro that I could muster and find this Capt. Harvey of the Texas Rangers.

We'd heard so many stories about the man by then. That he was Leif Ericson personified. That he had been educated at Yale and declaimed Burns freely on the march. That he was still in love with a dead woman named Laura or Lorie or Lorelei and that this gave him his tragic air. Some of my ladies were a little inclined to find husbands again, I suppose, forgetting propriety altogether, and I suppose these stories fulfilled them in a way that loving arms no longer could. I admit that I had read too much Sir Walter Scott in my day, *Waverly* being a particular favorite. So I secretly wished for this Cat Harvey to be of Highland stock and build. Shelley tells us that poets are the unacknowledged legislators of the world, but I know now that he must have been talking about warrior-poets and nomadic chieftains. Only a silly thing still in her girlhood would believe someone as sickly as Keats could force back a Yankee.

Yet when we encountered Capt. Harvey for the first time at that fired bridge to the Little Ohoopee River, our chieftain looked as skinny and underfed as any other boy-soldier. His very presence took all the romance out of our journey. Yet I, if the rest of the ladies did not, saw something dilate in his emerald eyes larger than his pupil, so as to eclipse them. He had a hard set of eyes, eyes that had once been kind. It made the rest of him appear exposed like a fresh wound. "Gaunted and haunted," Mother would say. It made my young widowed heart leap out to him, though I knew he was dangerous, like wanting to pet an adolescent tiger like a kitten.

We tried to leave him. I realized that once we chose him there would be no turning back. He would be ours. We would be his. So we slunk out in the middle of the night and set to ride north ourselves. What did we need Cat Harvey for? Did he not flat tell us that he wouldn't lead a "side-saddle cavalry" into battle? And yet we found ourselves falling in with more widows on their way to Savannah, as if all thirty-three of us were somehow swept up in Cat Harvey's tidal flow until we reached the field of battle. But, oh, what a glorious battle it was! Widows on a hilltop with a little drummer boy beating a Highland march in 7/8 time. We didn't need a directive. We had but one objective: kill Yankees and save our chieftain below. It was the first time I fired my guns at another human being, Yankee villains though they be. I gave a full-throated Rebel yell and poured so much lead into them it was a wonder that I had never taken up arms before May 14, 1865. It was sheer poetry. In my ecstasy, I accidentally shot Capt. Harvey in the arm. But God in his Providence let him live!

Now we are on the march with our chaperone. I am the farthest I have ever been from home. But my home is ashes now. And soon, very soon, so will William Tecumseh Sherman's be.

POLK INGRAHAM

He walks and talks in his sleep, my cousin does. And nobody knows this but me. They think he stands picket in the night. That he never sleeps. But I know the truth. I know that Cat is dead to the world, though his green eyes might seem open, and his body might stay alert to yours. He can hold an entire conversation with you in his sleep, but that's not my Harvey cousin what's talking. It's Cat and the witch what's riding him.

I'm an Ingraham and he's a Harvey, but now that feud business is over—and good riddance. Cat's my blood kin and I'll stand by him, right or wrong. Yet I cain't help feeling like the Devil's got hold of my cousin somehow and won't let him go. He airn't been the same since Persey Wallenger rid over that torpedo near Savannah and blew hisself up, with Cat riding right beside him when the road exploded and flung pieces of Persey into the lowest branches of the nearest tree. Cat's been walking and talking in his sleep ever since.

We have camped near Dover between the Ogeechee and some railroad tracks twisted into Sherman neckties. I have never seen this many widows bunched together in my life, nor so many gals wearing the widows' weeds for that matter. They saved our lives in Savannah. We were goners for certain. But now I wonder what my cousin plans to do with so many wild women. I was raised to protect ladies from danger, not let them shirl into the fight. But these widows are a stern and resolved set. They don't act like ladies, no matter how dainty they seem. They act like some of the women what pressed the frontier. They all want to clean their guns or sharpen their knives and talk endlessly about when they might could burn Gen. Sherman's home down to cinders.

I know I'm still a shavetail kid (Cat and Worth don't tire of reminding me this). I may be fifteen, but I still fought in Bentonville in the Rangers' last charge, and I can stand picket all night without falling asleep. And I can ride this country like a sure enough Injun and level my shotgun quick as thought.

But what I cain't seem to do is wake my cousin up when he stalks a night like tonight.

Cat is balanced on the balls of his feet staring towards the river. If I don't stand in his way, he'll try to cross it in his sleep. So I step in front of him, though not too close. He looks right through me.

"Cat," I say. "Wake up! You're dreaming agin!"

"Cat is in," he says. "I was Handsome."

"Cat," I say. When I reach to put my hand on his shoulder to shake him awake, he grabs it and flings it back.

"Stop calling me that," he says.

"Cousin," I say. "Come back to camp."

But it's like he don't hear me. Instead, he says, "I'm still dreaming about my former life. And you are just a dream. Cause when I awaken, I'll be in the twilight again."

"What twilight, Cousin?"

"A place where you're a number," he says, "not a name."

BRIANNA O'QUINN

WE CHOSE HIM. The blow-in from Texas. He dinna choose us. What would a peevish lad like our captain want with a bevy of Dublin widows riding muleback? Some with muskets so old that even the dogs in the street know they were unfit for battle. I was after wearing the sheriff's star on my full mourning dress. The Dublin men tried to put lies on me, the cowards. Said it was I that killed my husband, not the War. They called me "Banshee O'Quinn" behind my back and said I would corrupt the young girls into dressing like men and smoking tobacco. It feigned me not a bit. The words you canna say to my face are mere gnats over a bog.

But I dinna take kindly the way Capt. Harvey traveled with a Gatling gun that we could clear as day use against the Yankee heathens. The way he refused our call to arms at first. I thought him a coward, like so many men that returned to town without a single scar on their bodies. I said as much without blushing.

Later, after we escorted the Rangers out of Dublin, Shannon said to me, "Perhaps we made an idol of the captain, and God has given us this man instead."

"You sound like a Presbyterian," I told her. No, I knew Cat Harvey be our chieftain. I could see that in his eyes, eyes as emerald green as my dreams of Ireland. So I gathered up my posse of twenty-six widows and left Dublin to fend for itself, wearing green, velvet elope hats with many carrying their forefathers' shillelaghs across their pommels. My Shelias and Shannons were anxious to ride north, find the heathen Sherman's home and burn it like hellfire. But an ineluctable force that I now know was the Holy Spirit seemed to put us on the Old Savannah Road and guided us to our first battle. And what a fine battle it was! So many armed young widows charging downhill on their steeds at full gallop. We gave a throaty Rebel yell and poured fire onto those heathen Yankees who shot too low to kill us. We rode like the warrior-saints of old. I suppose I probably cried real tears as we so-called ladies emptied the saddles of our enemy. The Archangel Michael was there. Several of my girls saw him that day. He steadied my hand as I emptied my sidearms and shot true every time. But before pride, the deadliest of sins, could corrupt my heart, the Lord Jaysus saw fit to guide my hand and take aim at the very captain we were meant to save. I shot him. God have mercy, I shot Cat Harvey in the arm. I nearly killed our chieftain! It hurt my pride, wounded it if not mortally.

I was too ashamed to admit I was the one who shot him. Instead, I commanded two of my lieutenants to tend to the poor lad. His own lieutenants in the meantime stood dumbstricken, having been delivered at the hands of stern and resolved widows; but not the captain. Even with the noose still round his neck and a flesh wound, Cat Harvey appeared the perfect specimen of calm. I felt it again, this time in the pit of my stomach. I should fear this man, though he be only a few years out of his boyhood. You should fear him, Brianna, like the Devil himself. When his eyes sized me up for the first time, a mere glance downward and back up, I suddenly felt naked in his presence. And when our captain gave me his first order—to swap out my mount and musket with the Yankee dead—I felt a chill go up my spine. I chose him and once chosen I felt compelled to mirror him.

What would Mr. O'Quinn say if he were still alive? The man for whom I wear the widow's black and yet do not grieve? I had just gotten used to the idea that my name was O'Quinn when he up and died at Knoxville, practically in my arms, in that makeshift hospital. I made the worst sort of nurse. I hadn't the soft touch. So when my man died, I cut my hair with shears, stripped off his uniform and took his place on the field of battle for the duration of the War. I played the role of Darby O'Quinn at Chickamauga, Chattanooga and Franklin. I spoke little, but my messmates knew I was a woman. They said nothing. I must have made the perfect tomboy to them, grunting my replies. They were defeated men, so what did they care if a woman was in their midst? They cursed Bragg, and then they cursed Hood. But we stood shoulder to shoulder and let the Yankees cut us to ribbons. Battle dinna make me strong; it just made me wise. But when I returned to my beloved Georgia that had been wrecked to pieces, I knew I couldna return to playing the Dublin lady. Up was down, down was up. So I decided to turn partisan, and I've been riding ever since.

We rise at sunup, break camp and water our horses at the Ogeechee before crossing it.

"What do you want, Irish?" he asks as I ride up. Not once has he called me by my Christian name.

"Did you sleep well then, captain?" I ask Cat Harvey on the march. Knowing that he spent another night circling the camp like a wolf. The girls are singing Rebel songs I do not care to sing.

"Sleep don't hurt," he replies without once looking at me. For all of life I canna tease the mystery out of the man.

"There be four more widows from Dover that joined us in the middle of the night," I say. "Whose should they be?"

"Tch," he says, practically spitting. "Four more mouths to feed." I want him to look at me.

"You sound disappointed, Captain," I say. "I should think they deserve welcoming." My Yankee horse, whom I've named Echu, plays his vagaries with me.

Cat turns to look me in the face and says, "Then that makes me a widow, too." I am told Cat Harvey has not been the same since his friend Persey rode upon a torpedo buried in the road and blew up beside him, flung into the trees. It dinna make him shaky though, but quite stilled. And from this stillness he adds, "Give them to Eliza. She lost two her gals the other night."

"Do you want my girls to scout ahead and find a place to camp?" I ask.

"No, Irish," he says. "I want the Dubliners kept in the rear. The post of danger, so the post of honor."

"Then who'll be—"

"This is why I don't like women on the march," he says. "Song-singing and chatter."

I turn Echu around and trot back to the rear with my girls. Sometimes Cat Harvey can be a right keen bastard.

SMIT HARVEY

WE FOLLOW THE river northeast until we reach a military installation near the hamlet of Millen just hours before eventide, the time when Catullus forgets himself and we can no longer recognize him. One of his spells, don't you know. He calls a council of war on a hill. Men only. So I must admit that it's still a man's war, even if we are outnumbered tenfold by angry widows who have learned to ride and shoot.

My little brother takes out his cracked Yankee spyglass and peers down at the little fort. He does not offer it to any of us. Instead, he folds it shut and says, "A hush gonna fall over Jerusalem."

No one speaks. I imagine Cat calls these councils of war as a matter of form. He has precipitously become "Capt. Harvey," and we find ourselves promoted to his lieutenants.

Then Worth Somersett says, baffled, "You aim to attack them with a bevy of widows?"

Cat nods his head once.

My little brother. Do not underestimate a Harvey. We are a proud race. But my little brother. The absurdity of it all. After the shell exploded beside him at Shiloh, Cat was a changed man. I saw my youngest brother age ten years after Shiloh. He also threw himself into battles with headlong fury. And when he rode with Shannon's Scouts and did God knows what in the name of war, as Sherman's March swept aside so many of us in Wheeler's cavalry, I could see that Cat's eyes betrayed horrific images that no boy his age should have seen. He was only fifteen when he went to war, don't you know. Perhaps Sul should have left him at home. But our brother had plans for Cat. I imagine so did the God of Battles.

The Yankees are oblivious. We not only own the high ground, we have the element of surprise. What Yankee in his right mind would believe that some Rebel could cobble together a battalion after Appomattox? Old men and children. That's who was left at the War's end. No, those unsuspecting Yankees could not imagine how many mounted and armed widows we have. All of them ready to die.

Polk and Worth wheel Big Ben, our Gatling gun, up to the hill and point him directly at the installation. I despise such weaponry, but Big Ben has proven useful in some very tight places. Now Cat reveals his plan, which we are meant to approve.

"On my command," he tells us, "Smit, you fire Big Ben at the guards. Polk, you feed him the ammunition. The rest of you will ride with me. We will form a close column; and when the Yankees come boiling out like ants from a hill, we attack them. That oak down there is the capital of our salient. That clear?"

"Gin clear," Worth says. The rest nod.

"Tonight we supper up on plenty of good things," my little brother says. "What all them Yankees have."

Then Cat picks two squadrons to lead himself. The Morton sisters with their Milledgeville widows form the first squadron, and Eliza Reed's Statesborough widows form the second. They all form in close column perpendicular to the oak at the bottom of the hill. No sooner have they formed then my little brother catches my eye, points to Big Ben and orders him to "Fire!"

I crank Big Ben and he rains bullets down on the guards, who fall instantly. Then I stop turning the crank. We all can hear a commotion coming from inside the fort. Then a Yankee squadron of troopers bolts out onto the grounds below. But Cat orders me to hold my fire. He stands up in his stirrups and yells, "Charge them, you Gott damn widows! Charge!" then drops into his saddle, spurs Snaps forward and leads his two squadrons in their attack. The widows let loose a Rebel yell, exorcising the demons in their throats. A dozen widow skirmishers deploy behind Cat, firing and galloping to the right and left. The Yankee troopers wheel about in confusion. They mass into a square just in front of the oak, trying to form a column. But now the Morton sisters' widows divide into two parts. One follows Vella to the left; the other follows Marietta to the right. When these two troops advance, Eliza's widows now start at a trot downhill. The Yankees fire at random, but manage to hit only two widows in Vella's charge. But once they open fire, the Morton sisters' Milledgeville widows discharge their own weapons at the massed, confused square of Yankee troopers. They empty many saddles. Meanwhile, the second column of Statesborough widows gallops and charges vigorously. By now Cat's skirmishers have closed in by degrees and at last take the head of the charge. The Yankees turnabout and endeavor to retreat to the fort, but the widows descend on them too swiftly. Only a lone trooper breaks free. I don't crank Big Ben this time. I rise and draw my revolver, take aim, and fire.

It is a massacre. Some Yankees attempt to surrender, but the widows ride under the black flag and shoot them dead. The few rascals who remained inside the fort attempt to bolt. But Big Ben mows them down. Cat and the widows ride into the fort, and now the rest of our battalion mount up and descend the hill, shouting in jubilation.

I am astonished. I lost my leg in Bentonville, don't you know. I thought that was an audacious charge. But what I have witnessed here is nothing short of miraculous. I clap my hand on Cousin Polk's shoulder and shout, "Huzzah!" Then we mount our horses and ride down to the celebration. Widows are wheeling out wagons loaded with supplies. One hands me a jug of fine Georgia peach brandy. I relieve her of it and take long drafts as I watch the orderly disorder take shape. One of the wagons contains a great quantity of *Vin Tonique Mariani*, a Peruvian wine that contains coca.

Then our little drummer boy, whose name escapes me, drumrolls out a steady march. He is so excited. The widows gather round and clap hands in time with Drummer Boy's beat. No sooner has the boy drumrolled for the sixth or seventh time, then Rainy Greer, our campfollower from San Antone, appears with his box-fiddle to accompany him. Rainy plays a wild, soaring reel, one we have never heard before. Yet all present cheer him on. It climbs so high I feel Rainy's box-fiddle must be a champagne bottle about to pop.

Then he suddenly stops and looks up at the fort.

We all turn our heads and see that my little brother now bears in his left hand a smoking pineknot. He makes no speech, though it is an occasion for extemporaneous oratory. No, Catullus simply takes his pineknot and sets fire to the fort. Slowly but surely, it goes up in flames. The widows ululate like Arabs, as Cat steps back to stare into the fire.

Some widows tell Rainy to "play *Dixie*" and even more agree. And Rainy is about to oblige them when my little brother silences them with his sudden gaze.

"No *Dixie*," Cat says, adamantly. "*Dixie*'s played out. I want *The Yellow Rose of Texas*."

VELLA MORTON

WE CHOSE HIM. God help us. The blamed manchild who needed us to save his sorry hide back in Savannah. We chose him.

Him. That Cat Harvey. Like to haul off and hit him. But my sister, Marietta, reminds me that it's slim pickins in 1865. What, with all the generals fagged out. Captains, too. Marietta says to me without saying a word that Cat Harvey is all we got, so better jine up with his cavalry or git left behind. But I like to haul off and hit him, he makes me so mad. After we burnt the fort in Millen, we rode up to Louville and camped on the Ogeechee. I ask him point blank, "Where do we ride next?" My Milledgeville gals were raring to fight agin.

You know what he up and says to me? Our captain tells me, "Wherever I decide."

Like to haul off and hit him. He was that smart-mouthed with me when he rode into Milledgeville with that Gatling gun and those kid coffins filled with gold. Like nobody knew he was hiding something in those coffins. Why else have a Gatling gun? He acted smart with me then. Calling me a "lady." Shit, I know I'm a lady. But I come to learn that when most menfolks call you lady what they really mean is shut the hell up. I can drop a curtsey good as any gal, but what the South needs in 1865 is a good woman not a useless prissy lady. You know some of our widows ride side-saddle? *Side-saddle!* Who do they think they are? Queen Victoria?

Mr. Morton tried to make me ride side-saddle when we was courting. I was a Scarborough back then. He said, "Miss Vella, why do you Scarboroughs ride like men?"

And I replied, "Cause Scarborough women can take it."

That made him blush. But I didn't care. He was courting me. I wasn't courting him. His brother married my sister first. Marietta hoped it would be a double-wedding, but Eli needed to think on it aspell. All the Mortons in Baldwin County, like as not, told him to leave Vella Scarborough alone. But he kept after me. Is why I married him in the end. He had grit.

Eli died of campsickness before he could even fight his first battle. I'm not ashamed to say I grieved the man. He deserved a better death.

Now I wear the widow's weeds in honor of him. By and by, when some in his family said that I need not wear them anymore, that I'd grieved Eli enough, I told them what I thought about that. I told them, "Black reminds me we're at war." I held back, too. What I ought to of said was, "My sex between my legs won't let me wear the gray, but I sure as hell can wear the black."

Cat Harvey is nothing like Eli Morton. Eli was hale and hearty. This captain of ours is scrawny. I can lick him, I bet. All the other widows hang on his every command, but not me. I'm waiting for him to die in battle, so I can take his place. (I already accidentally shot him once, back at our first charge in Savannah.) I don't need to be called "captain" neither. Vella is fine by me.

It's his staring eyes. Like grass, those eyes. They seem to ignore you most of the time, then: there they are, looking at you. Never had a look bother me like that, the first time he set his eyes on me. They looked right into my soul. Like to haul off and hit him right then and there.

Now his eyes are on me agin. He has jined me by my picket post by the river. The night is not half as dark as his stare. He can see in the dark, I come to find. Cat holds a bottle of *Vin Mariani* in his hand. I wait for him to talk.

"Marietta," he finally says.

"I'm Vella," I say. "Marietta has blond hair."

"Awright," he says. "Vella then. You and your sister rode good in Millen. Good fighting back there."

"I know we did," I tell him. "I was there."

"You widows are full of sass, airn't ya?" he says, chuckling to himself. He uncorks the bottle with his teeth. "You drink?" he asks.

"Just in the morning," I say, guarded.

"My brother is a drunk, you know," he says. "I, on the other hand, have never swallered so much as a drop of alcohol."

"Baptists?" I ask.

"Presbyterian," he replies. "But that was a long time ago." He studies the bottle aspell.

"Why start now?" I say. "I know folks that don't drink. They like it like that."

Cat says, and this I'll not forget, "It's cause the nostalgia in me. I cain't keep it down." Then he takes a calm swallow of the wine. "So this is the blood of Christ?" he marvels.

"Well," I say. "That's that." I want him to leave me alone and let me stand picket in peace. I watch our captain take a big gulp this time. He stares across the river. For the life of me I don't know why.

Finally, he asks without looking at me, "You believe in ghosts, Vella?"

"I reckon so," I say.

Cat Harvey takes another swig of wine and says, "I think it's bullshit."

I don't reply in kind. He drinks more wine and I expect him to start slurring his speech any minute now, but instead Cat somehow grows more alert. His words, more fixed.

"Lost a brother in '62," he says. "During the evacuation of Nashville. Know how he died? Exposure. Pneumonia. Probably still be alive if Johnston would of let us fight it out back there."

"I lost my Eli to the typhoid fever."

"Then you *know*," he says. It struck something in my heart I hadn't felt for four years. I began to cry. So I turned my face away.

"Don't be ashamed," he says. "Wish I could cry. Would be better if men could cry, the way you women can."

"Please leave me alone," I say. My eyes still leak tears. "I need some privacy."

"No privacy in this army," he says. "We's all family now."

"You're not my kin," I declare. (Why won't my eyes stop leaking!)

"Blood'll let you down," he says. "No, we's a family what's better than blood."

"You're drunk," I say.

"I thought I would be," Cat says. "I thought I would be. But this tonic is stronger than coffee. I'm steady," he says, holding out his hand palm down. "See?"

My eyes finally quit and I wipe my face with my sleeve.

"You wish me dead," Cat declares, calm. He finishes his bottle. "I can tell. I seen that look before. You want me dead, Vella Morton. But you won't kill me yourself."

"I don't want you dead," I say. "I want to burn Sherman's home down to the ground."

"What did Tecumseh Sherman do to you?" he asks.

"He burnt Georgia, fool."

"No," Cat says. "What did he do to *you*?"

I think about that time I wish I'd forget. How I could of shot that Yankee if only I'd of got to my gun in time. How he didn't have the decency to shoot me afterwards, when he was done. How I just lay there with a full mourning dress bunched up to my thighs.

"Do you want me to come out and say it?" I say.

"You just did," he says. If he so much as reaches out to touch me I'll shoot Cat Harvey point blank. But instead, he stands still. He says, "Tecumseh Sherman took my mercy away. He took it away and now it's lost."

"Good," I say. "Then let's burn his home first."

But Cat shakes his head. "You widows," he says. "Burn Sherman. Burn Sherman. That's all I hear from you. Your hate is still too raw, like raw dough. I'm gonna leaven y'all into bread. The body of Christ."

"That's blasphemy," I say, though I only pretend to take offense.

"So is this," he says. "When Tecumseh Sherman marched on Georgia and through the Caroliners, all I heard from folks was that Jesus would intercede. That God was wrathful cause we made an idol of our generals, but

Jesus would intercede. Calm an angry God. But I seen Jesus, Vella Morton. It's true. I seen him hanging on his cross in a Georgia cornfield what the bummers burnt. A murder of crows hovered over his body whilst he just hanged there and let the wide world burn. Man thought that God had become flesh, but I tell you that Jesus was stuffed with straw what burns easy. God had sent His only son to burn in a Georgia cornfield. He had made Jesus a man, but not a man of honor. He let it happen to him. Just went up in flames on the cross. Nothing could resurrect him. He were no phoenix. He were just another scarecrow like the rest of us."

"And you believe that," I say.

But he says, "There are wrongthings, Vella. Those things you do not do. Unnamable things what the War brung out in us. What leaves you unclean. If there be such a thing as Redemption in this Christless world of 1865, then how does a man git shut his sins long enough to find it? How much repetition does a body have to take fore the body is played out?"

I say nothing. It is like the wine has made him exact, not drunk. I have no answers for him.

Then he says, "We shall burn the homes of all those Scouts what burnt y'all's homes. By the time Sherman will git word of it, it'll be too late. Then we'll make his wife a widow with nothing but a brick chimney left to remind her of hearth and home. We'll do it together, like family should."

I listen to the silence following Cat's words. I feel him looking at me through the night. *This man is crazy*, I think. But as soon as I think it, a bond is born. Our lives are intertwined, mine and his. I want to reach out and touch him, but Cat Harvey turnsabout and disappears back into the anonymity of camp.

I lift up the revolver in my right hand and rest it over my heart.

EUSTACE McCLINTOCK

I'VE SEEN SIGHTS. Fought in the War of 1812, and I've seen sights. A man don't have to leave Greensboro much to see the world. You live long enough, the world will come to you. I reckon I'd forgotten that war makes the angels strange. Heck, I thought this war was all played out. Wasn't there a Yankee garrison in Washington, not twenty miles from my home? I'm a Union man. I didn't fight against them British bastards just to watch my beloved America go into the hellhole of secessionism. I would have joined up with the Union, too, if they would have let a codger like me enlist. (If I weren't confined to this here chair, like I am—)

But nothing could prepare me for the sight of a whole bevy of widows on horseback and muleback, riding with guns of every variety on their persons. Some wearing slouch hats, like they're men. One even tips her hat to me as she rides past my cabin.

"Zeb!" I shout. "Zebulon!" My great-grandson steps onto the porch. "Bring me my musket!"

I didn't fight for my country just to watch a whole mess of widows keep up this damn Rebel nonsense. Zeb brought me my musket. I took my time loading it. My hands shake now, so I don't load as quick as I once did.

Before I have it fully loaded and can take a shot at one of those widows, a boy little older than Zeb comes riding up to my porch on a fine bay charger. He wears the traitor's gray.

He raises his hands up at me and says, "I surrender."

I don't like sass. I tell him, "Get off of my property." Once I have the musket loaded I swivel the wheels on my chair to take my shot. But damn it to hell, I drop my musket and it bangs on the porch. Zeb reaches to pick it up for me, but that's when the sassy boy on the charger pulls his pistols.

"Let's leave the musket alone, son," he tells Zeb.

I wait to see what this boy will do next. The procession of widows continues behind him.

"Sir," he says. "My name is Lt. Cat Harvey of the Texas Rangers."

"What the hell you doing in Georgia then, son?" I say. If I were only twenty years younger, I could drop down and pick up that musket and gladly die a Union man.

He has the audacity to smile at me. This Cat Harvey says, "Heard tell there's a man by the name of Eustace McClintock what lives in these parts."

"I am he," I say. My jaw jutted out like a proud veteran.

"Would you be the same McClintock what fought in the War of 1812?" he asks.

By now the procession of widows has all but disappeared. Now their wagon train rolls by.

"I am he."

"Well, sir," this Cat Harvey says. "I just wanted to git a look at you, is all."

If I could only reach my musket. If I could only just rise up from this chair and leap off this porch.

"Just what do you think you're doing with those widows?" I finally say.

This Cat Harvey turns his bay charger to the side so that they now stand in profile of me. Then he has the temerity to say, "I heard tell you're a staunch Union man, sir. I reckon you earned that right. So I'll tell you. These widows of mine are marching up north. Gonna raise some hell on Tecumseh Sherman's doorstep. Hell hath no fury and all."

If only I could just reach down. I say, "So what does that make you, Cat Harvey?" (I won't call no traitor to my flag "lieutenant.")

"That makes me their chaperone," he says, then turns his horse about and brings up the rear just when I spot the Gatling gun attached to one of the wagons.

Once they clear out of sight, Zeb picks up the musket to hand to me. I wave it away.

My great-grandson asks, "What was that, Paw-paw?"

For the life of me, I don't know what to tell the boy.

ELISHA TOOKE

We chose him. God as my witness we did. He looked nothing like a Texas Ranger neither when he and his scanty few men passed through Sparta weeks ago with their Gatling gun. None of that Texas swagger I axpected to see. He tried to rouse the Spartan men into lighting out west with him. To fight in Texas. I thought him crazy. Cat Harvey'd hardly growed a beard cross his face, and here he was acting like a man. I had questions he wouldn't answer proper. How would he arm his army, how would he feed it? He told me the God of Battles would provide. God of Battles? Hmmph. I'm sick to death of praying to the fickle God of Battles.

And yet do I follow.

It was Cat's eyes that I couldn't git out of my head. Most of the Spartan men that returned from the War had dead eyes. Not Cat's. They were crows-footed, too, but still green like a frog that hops fresh out of a river. I like feist and fire in a man. And Cat's eyes told me that he had plenty left in him. But at first I ignored the call. I'd lost all my menfolk in the War. I reckoned that Cat Harvey would die soon enough. That that was the last we'd hear of him. But then news reached Sparta that a mess of Yankees got slaughtered outside Macon. Said it was a Gatling gun that did it. This stirred up my widows.

"It's him!" Ima Jean said to me. "The Texas Ranger!"

"Probably dead by now," I told her and the rest of my widows. Up till then, they'd looked to me to show them a way out of this mess. I don't know why. I have a mouth on me, is all. None of us had lost our homes, like the rest of the country, but we hated Yankees all the same for killing off our men. And we hated, I mean *hated*, General Sherman. Now they looked to me for guidance, even though I'se barely twenty-two.

"Probably dead," I told them again. "Or will be soon. He's doomed, ladies. Cain't you see?"

But they wouldn't see. We're a democracy of widows, and I seen plain as day that I was outvoted. It's like when my menfolk scrambled over each other to go to war. Brothers, cousins, even my father. When Mr. Tooke told me, "Darling, I have to go," I didn't cry. I knew my husband was pledged to go git himself killed. I axed him questions he had no answers for, but in the end I was resigned, like a good Christian, I reckon.

So we set out to find this Cat Harvey of the Texas Rangers. All twenty-eight of us. Our command joined other widows from all over the state it seemed, heading southeast. We found our captain with a noose around his neck outside of Savannah. One of our scouts had heard an axplosion, the torpedo that nigh killed Cat Harvey. Otherwise, we would of never found him, I reckon. We gave our first battle that day. I don't suppose there ever was a cavalry charge of widows like that in all of human history. The only mistake I made was accidentally shooting Cat in the arm. I know it was me that did it.

Now we're on the march. Widows join up every day in two's and three's. Some desert us. Not many though. The War has made us itching for a fight up north.

We cross the Oconee River and head for burned Atlanta. The widows sing Rebel songs all day, all axcept *Dixie*. Cat Harvey says not a word. We pass through blighted country that Sherman had torned up and burned. We finally camp on a branch of the Ocmulgee just outside of Oxford. It is not yet sunset when the captain pulls me aside.

"Mrs. Tooke," I insist he calls me. "You got concerns. Let's hear them."

I don't know how the man knows me, but he does. I proceed to list every concern I can think of, including how he axpects us to pass through burned Atlanta when there is for certain a Yankee garrisoned there. "Do you axpect us to fight a whole garrison?" I ax him.

But he up and axes, "Do you believe in the mysteries of Providence, Mrs. Tooke?"

Was this a trick question? I answer him honest. I say, "No."

"Do you believe Jesus Christ died for our sins?" he axes.

I answer him honest. I say, "I don't know anymore. What does that have to do with the price of beef or gitting us through a burned, garrisoned city?"

The sun is about to set. Cat gits this woebegone look in his eyes, which fill up with twilight. He doesn't answer me. Instead, he answers himself. "I used to believe," he says. "Till I lost my soul at Shiloh. It's been three years wishing I had it back. That's all my prayers are now, Mrs. Tooke: wishes."

He stares at the sunset. It's the first time I've seen him scairt. He looks like a little boy. Something tugged at my heart. My heart hurt for him.

I say, "My prayers don't amount to much neither."

"And yet we both pray," he says.

"Habit, I reckon."

"When we burn the homes of Northrop's Scouts," he says. "When we burn down Tecumseh Sherman's home, I reckon our prayers will be answered then. We'll force God and his haughty angels to answer to us then."

WORTH SOMERSETT

I<small>T'S</small> <small>BECAUSE</small> <small>THEY</small> killed my best friend, Scip. The reason I'm riding north with this battalion of widows. That, and the gold. There must be $300,000 in those coffins. But Cat won't pay us out. He acts like it's his gold, not ours. Like we didn't all discover it together on Secession Hill. He already whipped me in a fair fight for trying to take some eagles for myself. But that's okay. I'll bide my time. Cat Harvey won't whip me again.

But it's because they killed Scip at Camp Douglas. They rode us into the prison, but before we crossed the gates one of the guards saw we had a nigger in our ranks and shot Scip dead. I carry a bone cross on my person at all times. And I carved the name of that guard who shot my best friend. His name is Alan Taylor. I don't care nothing about burning Sherman's home. Let it stand for eternity, for all I care. When the time comes I'm lighting out for Chicago, where I'll find Alan Taylor and slit his throat with my bowie and let him bleed out under my watch.

I act like I miss Kentucky, like I miss my sweetheart, Anna Leigh. I haven't seen neither of them for over a year now. But if I'm honest with myself, I know I don't miss them much, I'm ashamed to say. The last time I saw her, Anna Leigh gave up her virginity to me. It was my first time, too. I looked at her different afterwards. I didn't think she was a whore for doing it, but my idea of her diminished considerably on the march. There was no more anticipation. I was satisfied, I reckon. But she acted like it was the end of the world. "Now you won't marry me," she kept saying, even though I hadn't yet proposed. "Of course I will," I told her. Felt like a lie. But I give my word. That still means something in 1865.

But it's because Alan Taylor killed Scip. I'll leave the treasure behind just long enough to settle that score.

We leave the Atlanta Road for to follow the twisted railroad tracks that lead nigh to the foot of Stone Mountain, where we camp. Cat calls another council of war. This time he includes some of the widows.

"We shall divide our battalion in two," Cat says. "I lead the first half around Atlanta cross the Chattahoochee to Marietta. Worth," he says to me, "you lead the second party into Atlanta."

"Why does he get to lead?" one of the widows demands (I think her name is Vella).

"Cause it's my prerogative, is why," Cat says. "Worth Somersett rode with Gen. Morgan into territory worse than Atlanta. That makes him your captain."

So I guess Cat promoted himself to lieutenant colonel.

I stare at Stone Mountain, shining in our firelights. It's like Cat wants to get me killed before I turn twenty. "What's in Atlanta?" I finally ask.

"Widows," he says. "Lots of them."

ELIZA REED

We didn't choose him. The Kentucky boy who looked on his new command with contempt. We chose Capt. Harvey, whom some of our girls now refer to as "Colonel." But since Fate has sent us our champion in the form of a slight young man, I'll not complain. He gave the order, so my Statesborough widows and I will follow this Worth Somersett into Atlanta, the belly of the beast.

When I first set eyes on Capt. Harvey, I knew he was our man. And I dare say I found him attractive, slight though he is. It startled me. I had not had thoughts like those since I first met Johnny Reed at an officers' ball. Johnny asked me to dance and, though he danced poorly, I knew I would fall in love with him.

I have not fallen in love with Cat Harvey.

But his eyes penetrate me. I find myself looking away. They are as green as the Devil's eyes. Yet mine are his complement. It matters little that Cat Harvey is a married man.

But I have not fallen in love with Cat Harvey. He does not meet my beau ideal.

His lieutenant, Worth, rouses us up before dawn. He tells me and the Morton sisters to saddle up our commands. We do so and light out just as the day breaks. It promises to be a lovely day, which causes me great concern. It was on a day such as this that I received news of Johnny's death at Antietam.

We commence singing *The Bonnie Blue Flag*, but Worth turns round and hisses, "*Quiet!*" I have always thought Kentucky boys were better bred. But clearly this one hates the sound of female voices on the march. He has told us nothing. He resents leading us—we can tell. I hope he deserts our battalion the first chance he gets.

We ride into Decatur, and it is here that Worth Somersett halts us. He flags the Morton sisters and myself to him.

"All right, widows," he says. "I don't know how to get women to fight. But you clearly do. Let's get some Decatur widows before we ride into Atlanta."

The entire town of Decatur is staring at us. It is a ruin. The men all wear their sidearms in the open. The ladies are mostly dressed in full mourning dress, as are almost all of us in the South. A man approaches our column and asks Worth, "What goes here?"

Worth looks back peevishly at his command and then tells the man, "Just chaperoning a few widows to Atlanta."

The man looks at Worth perplexed. He turns about and leaves us be. But now a Decatur widow approaches the column. She asks Worth, "Are you him?"

"Ma'am?" Worth says. He is dense when it comes to our Cause.

"No," I say to her in answer. "But we ride with him."

The widow says, "Is it true what they say? That he'll burn Sherman's home to the ground?"

"*We'll* burn it," Vella says to her. I nod in agreement. The widow nods back. She leaves us.

No sooner do we proceed than fifteen armed widows ride behind us. One rides alongside a pleading father or uncle.

"It's a sin!" he tells her. "Widows on horseback riding like cavalry!"

"You can go to Halifax then!" she tells him. This stops him in his tracks. He looks to the rest of Decatur for a witness. All the men seem to do is scratch their chins in wonder. Men. What are they still doing alive?

Our introductions are kept brief on the march. We ride until we come upon a Yankee checkpoint on the outskirts of Atlanta.

"Don't nobody get itchy trigger fingers," Worth says. "Not a shot fired, unless I give the order."

The Yankees standing guard look upon us as if we are circus freaks. I keep my right hand on my holster. I could shoot them on the spot.

"Halt!" a Yankee finally says. "What's the meaning of this?"

Worth says to him, "Shoot us or move out the way."

"What?!" the Yankee says as we ride past. The rest of those villains stare without raising their weapons.

Worth turns to me and says, "You, Eliza. Give us a Rebel song."

I commence singing *The Bonnie Blue Flag*, and the girls all join me. We ride through the checkpoint without a single shot fired.

The city appears before us like an ancient ruin. Sherman did this. In Atlanta, we don't even need to declare ourselves. We simply wend our way through the city, singing Rebel songs. The entire Yankee garrison stares on. They have never seen such a sight. They may have outlawed the wearing of the gray, but not the black. They don't know what to do.

A Yankee major rides up to us and shouts at Worth, "Disband this demonstration *immediately!*"

We continue singing. Worth says, "This is no demonstration, major. We're just passing through on our way to Marietta."

Vanquished, the major turns his horse around and whips him to beat a hasty adieu. Meanwhile, the widows seem almost as though they have risen from amongst the rubble. Two, then three, then seven. We welcome each one. Soon, there are twenty. We have not even reached our midpoint. We lose count after thirty-six.

A former soldier dressed in butternut rags tries to join our command. We protest. "Widows only," some of us say.

"Mister," he says to Worth. "I'll dress in widow's weeds if it means taking a shot at that bastard Sherman!" The widows break into applause. We allow him to escort us out of the city, as we sing *The Yellow Rose of Texas* in honor of our champion, Col. Cat.

But I have not fallen in love with Cat Harvey. I cannot afford to love another soldier.

JOHN HENRY HOLIDAY

W E HEARD ABOUT him all the way down in Valdosta. The Texas Ranger who took all the widows away from Savannah to Atlanta. The Texican who aimed to burn Sherman's house and steal Lincoln's body, too. Mama was sick again with the consumption. We thought she might die. So she demanded we take her back to Griffin. We traveled north through burnt country so's she could die with her people, she said. But Mama didn't die. We had to wait. I couldn't stand it. All the boys in Spalding County had fought in the War but me. Most were dead, but the ones that weren't heaped abuses on me and called me *chicken*. I fought every one that said it to my face. I didn't care how old they were. No one calls John Henry Holiday *chicken*.

But I couldn't stand it. I had to run away. I dared two of my friends to come with me. We snuck out in the middle of the night and lit out for Atlanta. But they got scared and turned back. So I was alone. I passed through the ruins of Atlanta easily. Nobody cares what a thirteen-year-old does since the Surrender. I heard tell that Col. Cat was in Marietta. So that's where I went. And I never looked back.

I found the colonel's camp behind a house that Sherman didn't burn. At first, the armed widows wouldn't let me pass through their pickets. They told me to go home.

"I am home," I told them. I guess those were the magic words.

Widows were everywhere: in the barn, in the smokehouse, in the milk-house, in the well-house. Some widows were teaching new recruits how to shoot. I never before had seen such sights. Then I saw the man himself: Col. Cat.

He was supposed to be taller. And strongish. But the Col. Cat I saw was only a little older than I. At first, I mistook the huge hulk of a man standing beside him as the colonel. But this was just Big Ugly, the colonel's bodyguard. Col. Cat looked like a dwarf beside him.

"Col. Cat," I said, but I garbled my words. I was born with a cleft palate and lip. The doctors operated on it, and I got the scar on my mouth to prove it. But it made me talk funny when I was a kid. Mama spent years teaching me to talk proper. But now I could hear myself sounding like a fool all over again. "I come to join the cavalry."

The colonel sized me up and down, then said, "No." Then he was about to walk off with Big Ugly.

I blocked his way. I said, "I come to join, Col. Cat!"

"Can you shoot?" he asked, like he was mad at me.

"I can ride," I said. It's true I couldn't shoot yet. I didn't even own a gun. Dad promised to take me hunting when I turned ten, but he had to go fight.

Col. Cat said, "Got no use for boys."

"I'm a man!" I declared. My speech seemed to get worse. "I'll whip anyone who says otherwise!"

Then the colonel laughed at me. He *laughed* at me. Big Ugly stayed absolutely still. Then the colonel said to him, "What do you think, Big Ugly?"

"Shavetail," Big Ugly said. So I balled my fist and threw it straight into his stomach. Liked to break my wrist it was so solid. But it made Big Ugly let out a single "uh." Then the ugly ogre smiled. So did Col. Cat.

"What's your name, son?" he asked me.

"John Henry Holiday," I declared.

"John Henry," the colonel said. "Can you groom a horse?"

"I can."

"Go find Uncle Calsas and tell him you're his apprentice. You listen to ever word he says. You sass him, he'll git mighty riled up."

"Yes sir," I said. I saluted him.

"We don't salute in this battalion," Col. Cat said. (I blushed crimson then.) "We's irregulars."

"Yes sir," I said, then marched to the barn to look for Uncle Calsas.

He was a *nigger*! The colonel sent me to apprentice myself to an old nigger! And he was like no other nigger I ever seen before. He dressed like a cowboy. He wore a bullwhip, too. When I entered the barn and realized who Uncle Calsas was, I lost the power of speech.

"What you want, boy?" he asked me. He somehow looked at me directly with his wall-eyes.

"Col. Cat…" I said. "Col. Cat wants me to tell you that I'm supposed to… that I'm supposed to apprentice myself to you."

He studied me with those wall-eyes. Then the nigger said, "I reckon not."

Never had a nigger contradict me before. I was about to grab something to beat him with when I seen that bullwhip on his hip again. Instead, I spat out, "But the colonel said!"

Uncle Calsas poked out his lip and snorted once. He said to himself, "Mr. Cat. Your huckleberry is beyond my persimmon."

I stood there waiting to learn my fate.

"Go grab you a brush, boy," he said to me. (He called me *boy*!) "You best learn how I like to brush mane."

I should have refused. I was raised to give niggers orders, not take them. But this was no ordinary nigger. Uncle Calsas was a mystery. I did as I was told.

Now we are encamped in the town of Big Shanty, where the Cherokees used to live. I groom horses and take orders from an old nigger cowboy who heaps abuses on me whenever I do something wrong. Ten more widows have joined our command.

I am the farthest I've ever been from home.

BEE BREWSTER

HE CHOSE ME. Though not the prettiest of my sisters, he still chose me. It happened in the cupola of my home, Brewster House. I had heard a noise that night, someone talking. If it had been one of my sisters who had heard it, they would have been frightened. They would have called for Father. But not me. I have always been brave, too brave. Though I should have been frightened, I lit a candle anyway and followed the sound all the way up to the spiral stairs to the cupola. That's where I found Lt. Harvey standing at the top of the stairs without his boots. I should have turned around. I should have called for Father. But I was a foolish girl then, too brave for her own good. I mounted the stairs and asked the lieutenant what was wrong.

I brought it on myself, you see. I somehow knew Cat Harvey was a monster, but I must have flirted with the lieutenant at the dinner table earlier that evening. His eyes should have told me, those green eyes. But I was still a silly girl then. I am a woman now.

I cut off all my hair afterwards, all my beautiful hair.

Father threw a fit. He slapped my face. He forbade me to leave Brewster House. My sisters wanted to know the reason why I sheared myself. I couldn't tell them. Finally, when I couldn't take it any longer, I told Father what had happened right under his own roof.

"No," he muttered to himself, thoroughly dumbstruck. "My daughter is still a virgin."

I told him again. I was such a fool back then. He beat me. I had no defense against him.

Afterwards, he said, "My daughter is still a virgin."

I knew right then that fathers can't protect their daughters; that they cannot even avenge them. By then, I had heard that the young widows of Milledgeville were gathering in the barn on the Morton sisters' land. News of a Yankee massacre had reached town and "Cat Harvey" was on every widow's lips. I defied Father. In secret, I sewed myself a full mourning dress. Once it was finished I raided Father's gun cabinet of the weapons I thought I'd need. I saddled his favorite horse, Fergus, and rode to the Mortons' land. I did not wear a bonnet either. I wore Father's black slouch hat.

I don't know whose name I heard more on the march to Savannah, Gen. Sherman's or Cat Harvey's. The Milledgeville widows cursed Sherman and praised "Capt. Harvey." So he is a captain now, I thought. Somebody made him a captain in 1865. Sometimes the widows sang Rebel songs, but I never did; I never even spoke once on the march, except when Vella Morton rode up alongside me.

"I know you," she said. "You're one of the Brewster daughters."

"Yes," I said, ashamed.

"What's a scalawag doing in this fight?" she demanded. "What's a scalawag Brewster that ain't never been married riding with widows?"

I looked at her, cold, and said, "Jack Brewster is dead to me. I think that earns me the right to wear black."

Now we are camped on the grounds of a Primitive Baptist church on Silver Creek. Cat Harvey is a lieutenant colonel now. He barely recognizes me, hardly acknowledges my existence unless I stand right in front of him. Then he tips his hat and says, "Miss Bee," as if that night had never happened, as if the awful memory of that night were mine and mine alone. I have already shot him once, during our first battle in Savannah. I wasn't aiming for him, but I know I shot Cat Harvey in the arm. But I wonder when I'm going to muster up the courage I once had and finish the job. I used to be so brave.

He leads as many widows who will follow him inside the white clapboard church. He brazenly steps up to the place where a pulpit should be and turns around to face us, like he is our pastor. We expect him to speak, but he waits. Cat Harvey reads the room with those impenetrable eyes I still seek to know. Then he places his left hand gently on his cheek and looks down at the floor.

"Widows," he practically whispers. "I am no hard-shelled Baptist. My people are Presbyterian. But I were married in this here church two years ago to my jewlarky, Lorelei. She married me, though I'd died at Shiloh on my first day of battle. She married a Rebel ghost. All of y'all are still married to your ghosts. Ghosts like me. We haunt your dreams and stalk your ever waking minutes. We's hungry ghosts, you see."

He grows solemnly silent for what seems like an age. None of the widows speak. They merely nod in agreement. Some even bow their heads to pray.

"Hungry ghosts," Cat says, then yells, "My wife is a widow, like you! She has suffered me mightily! The last she seen of me were when Columbia burnt under Tecumseh Sherman's gaze."

At the mere mention of Sherman, this rouses the church. A widow cries, "Hang him! Hang Sherman!"

"And we will!" Cat shouts. He gesticulates with wild abandon. "We'll set fire to all of Yankeedom for making ghosts of our men and widows of our wives! You prayed to the God of Battles and he answered you with a pitiful scarecrow called Christ, what burnt just as easy as the Georgia corn-field he were sent to protect!"

A widow stands up and shouts, "Blasphemy! And in the house of God!"

Yet before anyone can answer, Cat Harvey outstretches his arms, making his body a crucifixion, and shouts, "Ay, blasphemy! Blasphemy! In the burning house of God! Tecumseh Sherman burnt our Gospel shops from Atlanta to Raleigh! And where were Jesus Christ? Where were that scarecrow of a Christ? He stood idle, *idle* by, on his burning cross!"

"He died for our sins!" another widow jumps up and exclaims.

"So now we're supposed to die for His?!" Cat Harvey cries, pointing to Heaven. "When the Devil has held High Carnival over this burnt and blighted land?!"

The same widow bursts into tears and cries, "You cain't mean what you say! Think of your soul!"

"I already been to Hell, sweetheart," Cat says. "At Shiloh. At Chickamauga. At a hunnerd different towns and cities! I already been to Hell— *and so have all y'all!*"

We all nod and some shout, "Yes!" If it weren't for the War, I would still be a virgin.

He throws his arms out again and shouts, "And what are you gonna do?! What're you prepared to do?!"

"Kill them!" I hear from over my shoulder. "Burn them!" I hear in front of me.

I begin to sob. I don't know why. I feel the entire church looking at me, but I don't care. His words are too cruel to remain in my head. His cruel deeds are too much to remain in my heart. Some widows beside me bunch around me and hug me. I don't want them to touch me, but I can't resist. I become one of them, a widow.

Then I hear Cat say my name.

"Look at her," he says. "Look at what I did to her. Miss Bee, come forward."

I don't want to go. I don't want to go to him. I cannot see clearly from all my tears.

"Come forward, Little Bee," he says. "We cain't hurt you now."

I feel myself rise and move forward, as though carried by the hands of widows. I want to kill Cat Harvey right there in this church. I have my hand on Father's revolver. But I also want to collapse into his arms. I can't decide which, not even when I meet the attacker face-to-face.

He turns to the widows and says, "Look at this specimen of persecuted humanity. See how she trembles. See how her hand wants to draw a rig on me and shoot me like a rabid dog. Who but me did this to you, Bee?"

"No!" I hear another widow shout. "Not you, Col. Cat!"

"Yes me," he says. "I had my wretched way with this gal in the cupola of Brewster House." Then Cat turns to me, and says, "Tell them Bee."

Instead, I draw my sidearm and point it against Cat Harvey's right temple. I cock it, but do not fire. I hear the myriad firearms of the widows cock at me. I do not care. If I die, I'll at least have killed the one who took my girlhood away.

He closes his eyes once, then opens them. Those eyes finally become clear to me. I see his pain. His pupil is a deep dark well of pain. And my fingers stiffen. My entire body freezes.

"Shoot me, Little Bee," he says. "Like as not, I'll hurt you again."

"Shoot!" he cries. "I'm dead already."

But I cannot take his life. I fail at the one task I'm pledged to accomplish. Then Cat Harvey reaches for me with those same hands that once beat me and ripped off my clothes, and embraces me. I have already dropped the gun by my side. I stand before the congregation of widows like a sinner called to the altar. I do not sob this time. I merely cry hot tears.

"Oh, Little Bee. Little Bee," he says into my ear. "I promise to give you back everthing what's been took from you."

He must be lying. I want to raise Father's revolver and fire it. But instead, I find myself crying into Cat's very shoulder. "How could you do that to me?" I want to cry. "Answer me!"

He somehow hears my unsaid words. Cat Harvey replies, "If I'd of knowed it would come to this… but that's just wishing."

Now I feel more hands on me. Widow hands. They embrace me, too. Cat and I become the center of a circle of widows. I couldn't raise my gun if I wanted to now. Cat Harvey married his wife in this church two years ago. But he has married me to the widows today.

UNCLE CALSAS

I'T'S GONNA BE some problems. I'm a nigga that been in this here war longer then I cares to know. I ain't seen Texas sky going on ten seasons now. Ain't seen my sweet Serena longer than that. Sometimes I git to feeling poorly over her. Too much salt in my sweet bread. Was a time, I played my mandoline whenever the missing her got too hard to bear. But they took my fretting hand away from me. I still feel my two missing fingers, like I still feel Serena's touch.

But it's gonna be some problems. A hush gonna fall over Jerusalem. What all with these here mad widows in our mitts. They ain't studying no Northrop's Scouts. They wants to burn Marse Sherman's home, like he did Georgia. Like the War still going on.

But I reckon not.

So why all I go north stead of lighting out west back to Texas? Cause I'm obleeged to go. I'm still a nigga and Lincoln is dead. Besides, I gots to protect Polk from Mr. Cat.

We ride through the seven hills of Rome and into town. This here nigga wid a Chinese gong comes out of a hotel, erbout to clang it for dinner, when he spot Mr. Cat and turns tail back inside. Like always, the widows be mustering up. But I knows for ever third widow that musters up wid us, one widow goes home. I reckon they thought twice erbout killing Marse Sherman. I reckon they remembers they's still wimenfolk.

It mean more hosses for me to shoe. And I gots nothing but a white boy for to apprentice.

I'se old. It take up a lifetime been a nigga. I don't ride natural like back when Texas was a country. But I can still break a hoss, even with only one good hand.

Mr. Cat says, "Saddle up. We's gonna press horses."

Then we ride into the country looking for what all good hossflesh be left in 1865. He bring me along cause I know how to speak hoss. No secrets betwinxt them and me.

We come upon this one plantation where all but two ole twin niggas'd remain put. They massa was away, the chatty one say. That nigga's name is Remus. I got no use for him. But he twin brother, Romulus, say to Mr. Cat, "Whar all you riding, Massa?"

"North," Mr. Cat say.

"Does you need a hand, Massa?" Romulus say. He brother say, "Romulus! How can you think of leaving this plantation when Massa is away?"

"Jimmy crack corn and I don't care," say Romulus to he twin. Which make Mr. Cat laugh.

Mr. Cat say, "We airn't pressing no niggers. Just horses."

"Need a cook?" Romulus ax.

"Nope."

"Need a blacksmith?"

"Got one already."

"Have y'all got a relater?"

Mr. Cat say, "What's a *relater?*"

"Oh," Romulus say. "He relates stories for whitefolks when they finish they supper."

Mr. Cat looks at me, like I might be a relater. I say, "I reckon not."

Then Mr. Cat say, "Can you ride a horse?"

"Nawsir, but I can run beside you."

Meanwhile, he twin shakes he head. He remain faithful. I reckon that's how they tell the difference betwinxt them.

So Mr. Cat say, "Follow me."

And like the rat say to the cat, that's that.

JINCY McBRIDE

I CHOSE HIM. I was never none too choicey. I come up in the Mountains. But once a mountain girl chooses her man, she cuts down on him directly. He kin go quiet or go noisy, but he's gonna *go*.

I chose him cause he married me without my permission one night in North Carolina not three months ago. Cat Harvey was purely rosined. But he catched me at my weakest. He drug me down, he driv up inside me, and married me like a brute. I scattered afterwards. We should of fought fist and skull, but I give in on him. He had me in a grab chain. Cat Harvey married me, and thar was nothing more I could do axcept find him agin and make him pay mightily.

I was so weak. I'd just lost the daughter in my belly, Ruth Ann, before the Surrender on the road to Virginny. I'd left the Mountain to go find my husband, Luther Earl, what the Home Guards had captured and dragooned into the fight. The Rebels needed men so bad, they drug mountain boys, like my Luther Earl, into they war. We'd just set ourselves to chapping when the Home Guards commenced dragooning us. I had to stow Luther Earl in a bear cave that winter, but when Spring come up directly, the Home Guards found him. Sent him off to fight and die in Virginny. I left out after him on foot. First I ever set foot off the Mountain.

I was too late. By and by, I miscarried Ruth Ann on the roadside. In North Carolina I fell in with a passel of refugees. Kind folks. I was afflicted with grief. I could still feel Ruth Ann kicking in my belly and told myseff that she was still in thar. That I refused to birth her till the world was set right agin. I was monstrous afflicted with grief. The refugees fell in with some Texas Rangers. Boys I paid no mind, axcept for Cat. He had these mysterious lush eyes. I didn't trust them. I minded those eyes.

But on the third night that we laid out with the Rangers, the Moon had stobbed me betwixt my legs all over agin. And I did bleed. That's when I seen that Ruth Ann was dead. I ran off not far from camp to grieve. That's whar Cat Harvey found me. That's whar the right bastard married me without my permission.

But I chose *him*. I regained myseff. And when I did, I struck his track. I didn't go back to the Mountain, though it would of been a comfort to me. I lit out for South Carolina, then Georgia, looking for Cat Harvey, the only other man what married me besides Luther Earl. It tuck me two months, but I found him. By then I fell in with some widows looking for the same man. Calling him a hero. (Iffen they only knew Cat Harvey like I.) But I said not a word. I was thar at the battle we give off in Savannah. I knowed it was I that shot Cat Harvey in the arm, not any other widow. I didn't aim to level my hog rifle at him, but I must of cut down on him just the same.

After the pearly gunsmoke cleared I told him what for. I said, "Hear me once—I won't say it agin. I found you, so now you're catched. Soon as we find a preacher, you're gonna marry me for what you did back in North Caroliner!"

That fox skunned the wrong henhouse.

Now the whole bevy of us rides north through the Chattahoochee forest. And I still ain't found no preacherman what will marry us proper. They flat refuse to marry a widow yet in black.

DARKISH LLEWELLYN

Like the circus come to town. I have lived in Ringgold all my life, but I've never seen such as the procession of widows that rode into town this morning. We had heard rumors, of course. That a brigade of widows rode under a Texas Ranger out of burned Atlanta and into the Chattahoochee forest. More Munchausen, we thought. City gossip. We were merely trying to survive 1865. Then this morning I studied the gray and black rocks in the hillscape by my home. I have eaten the clay between those rocks. Good dirt. So I know when there is a disturbance up ahead. Just like I knew before anyone else in Ringgold that Sherman was coming. It's written in the rocks.

I tried to warn the town, but the townfathers (what was left of them) didn't take me seriously. I was Cassandra all over again. I stood on the corner of Maple and Nashville Street on the courthouse square. "Something's coming!" I yelled. "Something's coming from the south!" No one would hear me, it seemed. I was still "that clay-eater, Darkish Llewellyn."

But the Ringgold widows did. Young and old, they gathered in front of the courthouse. The young widows had mounted their mules and horses. Some brought their Negro wenches. They wore men's hats and carried weapons of every variety. But the old widows had come out to scold them. One said to me, "Darkish Llewellyn, look what you started!" But the young widows didn't care. They waited, and sure enough, we saw birds fly from the mountain forest in the distance over our brick buildings from the south. And soon we saw a little drummer boy dressed in a baggy butternut uniform. We heard him roll on his drum and beat out a Highland March. He was alone for a very long time as he circled our square. The men in the town went indoors, the cowards. But the widows, young and old alike, waited.

Like the circus come to town. We heard fiddle music. We heard clapping and singing. Then we spotted him, the man himself. Col. Cat Harvey, riding a bay charger beside his huge ugly bodyguard at the head of a column of widows. He was just as I had seen him written in the rocks. A slight man no older than myself. His blond beard rambling across his face, clearly the first one he ever grew. But there was an aura about him, something in his eyes. I imagine that's why I stayed. I imagine that's why I followed.

Some of the Ringgold widows still listened to their widowed mothers. They reluctantly left the square with their mothers walking their horses, holding the reins. But the balance of the Ringgold widows remained put on the courthouse square, as Col. Cat circled it until we were all surrounded. Then all singing ceased.

Col. Cat tipped his hat to us, and said, "Morning, ladies."

"Are you him?" Susannah Carter asked, like a hopeful child. "The Texas Ranger?"

"I'm a pilgrim," he said. "On progress from this world to that which is to come."

"Satan!" one of the mothers pointed and cried. Some of Col. Cat's widows leveled their shotguns at her. But he waved them away.

"No, ma'am," he replied, pleased. "I'm the hungry ghost of Cat Harvey, what died in 1862 on Shiloh field." And he made two horns with his left pinky and index finger, like a sign of the Devil.

Then the old widow who had denounced the boy colonel fainted. No one picked her up, not even her daughter. He was like no man we had ever seen. We had seen plenty of sick and wounded men during the War. Ringgold's warehouses and hotels served as hospitals for twenty thousand souls. But this boy colonel had invisible wounds that he wore like a badge of honor.

"You know why we're here," he said. "You know where we heading. Jine up with us, or don't. I care not a whit."

He was about to put spurs to his bay charger when he noticed me in the crowd. I realized then I was the only white woman not wearing widow's weeds.

"What's your name, darling?" he asked.

"Darkish Llewellyn," I whispered. I don't know why.

"Why come you don't wear black?"

"Because I'm not a widow," I said. It was true.

"But you're a daughter of the South," he said.

I nodded.

"That makes you widow enough," he said. Then he put spurs to his charger and rode forward. They left the square riding north, towards Chattanooga, we imagined. And all the young widows and even a few old ones left too. They simply fell in. That's when our men began leaving their brick stores to chastise them. I watched the men foam with hate. But none would do more than let loose a volley of curses. Words. I had just about enough of men's words. I watched as the last wagon wheeled past me, and all of a sudden I clambered up into it. I had no gun; I had no horse or mule; I wasn't even a widow. But I jined up that morning as if my whole family had been wiped clean off the earth.

Now we camp on Chickamauga battlefield. The rocks cry out. So many dead here. Makes me so nervous I proceed to leave the campfires, walk past the pickets and dig in the dirt until I find a raw hunk of clay. Once I taste the cool, sweet clay I know that the blood in the soil has not yet seeped into it.

"You eat clay," I hear over my shoulder. I turn around and it's the colonel squatting on his haunches. I don't know how he can see me, it's so dark. I look downcast. I hide the clay in my hands. But Col. Cat says, "Don't be ashamed, Miss Darkish." (He still knows my name.) "Lots of folks eat clay now."

"I cain't help myself," I finally explain. The rocks cry out. They warn me that the colonel will hurt me. But I don't run. I am not sufficient enough afraid.

"You don't hate Tecumseh Sherman," he states as a matter of fact. "I can tell."

"I don't believe in hate," I finally say.

Col. Cat rises and for a moment I cain't even see him, not till he speaks. "When this campaign is over, Miss Darkish," he says, "you'll come to despise me."

HANDSOME

I AM NOT A number, I am not a slave; I am Henry Clay Somersett, the ghost damned to haunt Cat Harvey. I dream I have awakened again. This time in Chickamauga. Three thousand souls haunt this piece of ground. They wonder what I am doing here. I am dreaming again, dreaming that I am still alive in 1865. I walk around in this body that is not mine, circling the camp, afraid for what might be out there past the pickets.

I had escaped the hell of the nightworld when I rose to face my enemy and shot myself in the head. It was my second suicide. I had seen my destiny written in my midnight blue bloodshadow. It was revelation. It was a horror. Mine and Cat's destinies were intertwined. I would have to relive my memories—the rapes, the murders, the whippings—we committed with Shannon's Scouts. I had only one card to play, or so I thought. Kill myself.

Which led me into the twilightworld.

There are too many ghosts here. They crowd me. "What are you doing here?" they demand, knowing I am not their kind.

"I'm Handsome," I tell them. I will not give my Christian name. Nor will I give out my wretched number: 05031971. But these ghosts know my sins, mine and Cat's. They demand we leave or our battalion of widows will not sleep.

"Go on, then," I say. "Haunt us."

I would rather Chickamauga ghosts haunt me than wake up once more in the twilightworld where I am made to work on "Oakland Plantation." From day-dawn to dusk-dark it is a wasteland; not a single oak stands. Yet we are expected to plant our crops there: cotton, tobacco, rice, hemp. There, I am "05031971," a shade, a number. Here, I am something of a human being; albeit one who stalks the night, desperate to relive his sins.

The Chickamauga ghosts attempt to haunt our widows, but these ladies are already haunted.

Then scissored out of the night comes a widow, Eliza. She is a plain but capable woman. She has followed me here. She holds an apple out, as if she were Eve herself. And like Adam, I take a bite and hand it back to her. She takes another bite out of the apple. I feel the need in me return.

"Leave me, widow," I tell her, though it is Cat's voice that speaks. "I am not myself."

"We know," she says. "We know you're in pain."

"No," I rejoin. "You think we are a nice man. But we cause the pain. Now leave us."

She reaches for my hair, to stroke it. But I snatch her wrist and bend back her arm.

"Ow!" she cries. "You're hurting me!"

But the need in me has returned. We strike a blow across Eliza's face and drag her to the ground. She struggles to rise back up, but we overpower her. She manages to push us away but we fall on top of her. We are the experts, myself and Cat. Eliza is the inexperienced one. She has forgotten her guns. She cries, "Cat!" and then cries for help. But I know that the Chickamauga ghosts are making too much noise in camp for anyone living to hear poor Eliza's cries. It is a wretched business. We make her one of our warwives. Now she cries without making a sound. If we had any mercy left in our heart, we would leap off of her. But we don't. We are beyond redemption. We are animals. Monsters.

Once I ejaculate inside her cold, cold walls only then do I feel the extent of my sin spreading across my back, enveloping me. I clamber off Eliza, who clamps her legs shut, clutches herself and proceeds to sing to herself a child's song I do not recognize.

"I'm sorry," I say. "I'm so terribly…" But Eliza just sings to herself.

Quick as thought, I awaken to the plantation bell clanging. The nightmare was true, but twilight is truer. I rise from my corn shuck mattress, still dressed in my uniform with the number *05031971* written on my breast pocket.

ELIZA REED

It was my fault. It was entirely my fault.

I should have left him alone. We always leave him alone when he crosses the picket and stalks the night. What could he be doing, I'd wonder. I had to go and see. So it was entirely my fault. I should have stayed behind our pickets. I shouldn't have sought him out when he was in that black state. Now Cat Harvey has unsexed me. And it is entirely my fault.

Nobody can know about this. No one can find out. I must never tell a soul. It would hurt our Cause. Widows would flee by the dozens and then where would we be? Alone. Left at the mercy of Yankees and Negroes. No, nobody must ever find out.

My maidservant, Salome, knows something is amiss. "You look mighty poorly this morning, Miss Eliza," she says. Camp is breaking before the dawn.

"It is my time of the month soon," I say. And this leaves her perplexed. Our cycles have been synchronous ever since we were playmates. She sees the bruise across my face. But Salome says nothing. She fetches some herb of grace. I want to tell her about what happened last night. I want to fall into her arms and cry. But I have been unsexed. Those days are over for me now. And here I found myself falling in love with him on the march. I cannot love this man, this animal. I must recognize the danger he brings and help him direct it against Gen. Sherman.

Salome insists I eat breakfast, but I want to starve myself to death.

And then he suddenly appears, like the dawn itself. I don't know what

I was thinking; that he would be too shamefaced to meet me, that Cat Harvey would hide his face under his Mexican blanket and never show it again? But no. He sat right beside me and proceeded to eat breakfast with me, not saying a single word. Any day before this one and I would have felt honored. There were already so many widows vying for his attentions. But this morning I feel uneasy in his presence. Does he not know? He must! I want to shout. But he doesn't so much as look at me. He merely "breakfasts up" right beside me while the jealous widows look on. I want to denounce him. I want to denounce our colonel in their presence. I want to lift up my dress, point down there and say, "See! See! Look what you did to me!" But I cannot. We have not yet crossed out of Georgia country. We have so far to go.

I must never tell a soul. Who would believe me? It was entirely my fault. I have fallen in love with a beast.

Cat sops up his tin plate with some hardtack and then says, "Saddle up." Like last night never happened. Maybe it hadn't? Was I dreaming that he raped me? Did I lose my faculties last night and now cannot distinguish reality from fantasy? But it *did* happen. I have the bruises to prove it. Immediately after it happened last night I ran to the nearest creek, sat in it and tried to wash myself clean. But you cannot wash the bruises on your body away. You cannot wash away the dirt left on your soul.

We saddle up and light out for Chattanooga. We have come so far, but still have a long ways to go. So what am I to do? The Cause is greater than what happens to my body.

He chose me.

ABSALOM CANADAY

THEY DARED ME I couldn't do it. All of Chattynooga liked to join them in the dare. Them Yankees. They heard I make fiddles, bow fiddles and box. When the Yankees come and took over the city, by and by, them right bastards strolled into my shop. Oh they's friendly with me, sure enough. Struck up a conversation.

Then one says to me, he says, "Your sign says you make fiddles of any size. That true?"

Is that true? Cain't he read the sign? So I says, "Yep."

"*Any* size?" he asks. The other Yankees was grinning.

"Or my name ain't Absalom Canaday."

Then he unfolds a piece of newspaper with foreign talk on it. He points to a drawing of a fiddle that takes two men to play it.

"Can you make us an *octobass*?" he says, grinning. They all commenced grinning together, chuckling too.

They dared me I couldn't do it. Not in words. But I know a dare when I hear one. So I say to that right bastard of a Yankee, "Not for free." I named my price in gold, and we shook hands on it. Then I got to work.

Is what I get for shaking hands with a Yankee. I spent hours, days, weeks, months working on that octybass. The first one failed me. So did the second one. So did the third. It took me sixteen tries to finally make a bow fiddle big enough for two growed men to play sweet music on. The whole time I kept thinking about wiping the grin off them Yankees' faces. I come close to giving up. But I did it.

By then the War was over. Them Yankees lit out and left a nigger garrison in their place. I ain't seen them grinning Yankees since. Last time I shake hands with a Yankee.

So all of Chattynooga had a big laugh at ole Absalom. I reckon that's how that Texas Ranger heard about me. I reckon that's why he come into my shop.

"Mister," he says. "I hear tell you got a bow fiddle what takes two men to play."

"Get out of my shop!" I yell, and I mean it. Sass. These boy soldiers is full of it.

"Hold up, hold up!" he cries. "I airn't here to gawk at it. I'm here to buy, if it's as big as some say."

I give him a good hard look in the eyes and see he's serious. But before I show him that what's been the bane of my existence these past months, I tell him, "I only take gold for it."

"I got me some gold, sir," he says. "Now let's see that fiddle."

"It's called..." I say, puffing up with my pride, "an *octybass*."

RAINY GREER

Maybe I am camp trash, like Cat says. All I got is my fiddle and my pride, my pride and my fiddle. Maybe I am crazy. Didn't Cat put me in a issylum back in Raleigh? I don't heap blame on him. I was out of my head. But now I wonder which-a one of us is crazy. I ain't never paid cash on the barrelhead for a fiddle that's so big you have to wheel it in a wagon and takes two men to play.

He says to me, in all seriousness, mind you, "Rainy, I got a fiddle I want you to bow."

We wheel the tree-sized fiddle into the Chattynooga square right in front of the nigger garrison. Cat has two hulking widows lift the big fiddle out while he remains standing in the wagonbed. He hands me a bow the size of a tree branch and says, in all seriousness, mind you, "Here."

"What all am I s'posed to do with this?" I ask him.

"You just saw these here strings. Let me do the rest." He stands in the wagon with the big fiddle's neck. I remain on the ground with its body. I don't claim to know a Texas Ranger's reasons. I just follow orders, camp trash or no. So I commence to sawing cross those three thick strings as if I'se sawing lazy cross a tree trunk.

It makes the eeriest of sounds. Like a cross between a bull roaring and a growed man moaning for mercy. I feel the vibrations in my entire chest.

It's a bull-fiddle, I decide. So I name him *Toro*.

All the townfolk come out to have a look-see. The nigger garrison does, too. Cat, in the meantime, fingers *Toro* while I keep a-sawing on him. My two hands liked to drop from my wrists, they's so sore. But they keep a-saw-ing. It's like when I play my box-fiddle for a little persimmon beer money. The spirit just moves me. I won't know just how sore I am till I'm done.

Then *Toro the Bull-fiddle* makes music.

Cat fingers *The Yellow Rose of Texas*, which I know by heart. Now I no longer saw *Toro*. I bow him like the bull-fiddle he is. And the townfolks… well, they's awestruck, along with the entire garrison. And there's widows amongst the crowd. Lots of them.

When we finish, my hands is practically bleeding from tenderness. All of Chattynooga liked to clap their hands off for us. I take a bow and am about to pass the hat, when Cat says, "Hold up, Rainy."

A widow yells, "Speech! Speech!"

But Cat Harvey says, "No speeches. All y'all know who I am. You know why I'm here." Then he whistles for the two huge widows to lift *Toro* back into the wagonbed and wheel it out. The nigger garrison don't know what to do. But the widows do.

One tells the man standing next to her, "You there, give me your shot-gun!" She just up and takes it from him. Then another widow strips off the sidearms of the man next to her. They don't ask them—they commence requisitioning weapons of all shapes and sizes. This makes the garrison nerv-ous. Should they open fire? Their white officer signals for them: No. Duly armed, the widows commence pressing horses from the menfolk. They protest some, but the widows don't hear them. One widow says to one of the menfolk, as she mounts his horse, "What use have you got with a horse, Nathan Buell? You're an infantryman, *or so you say!*"

Toro the Bull-fiddle has stirred something up in the pit of them Chat-tynooga widows' stomachs. That's when I decide *Toro* makes a mating call to wild women. I pledge to keep him clean and finely tuned. It's about time I find me a widow to marry.

BRIANNA O'QUINN

I<small>T IS A</small> heathenish thing to worship rocks. But Darkish, the clay-eater, says that there is a waterfall inside Lookout Mountain. She's a jackdaw among peacocks. And Col. Harvey believes her. Why we are encamped on a mountain, only the Lord Jaysus knows. "To listen to the water inside the rock, Irish," the colonel tells me. Damn Darkish Llewellyn. The teeny girl-child clay-eater of a Welshwoman.

My Dublin widows have adjusted smartly to the march. We have only lost three of our number, the cowards. But our ranks swell so much that I am promoted to first lieutenant. And so I am. Col. Harvey has made his Texians our superiors, despite their weaknesses. Men. What are they good for?

Cat Harvey is in his lone. He stalks the night past the pickets, to howl at the moon, one supposes. But I have serious matters to attend with him. How will we feed all these widows and their horseflesh? What will we do with deserters? Serious matters. So I follow him past the pickets to the edge of the mountain. At first, I don't see him; it is too dark yet.

But then I hear from over my shoulder, "What're you doing here, Irish?"

I whip round and face him. He looks like he's stinking drunk. (Has he been nipping at that *Vin Mariani* again?) I brace myself for an attack from my own colonel. He does not move.

I say, "I must speak with you, colonel."

"I'm Handsome," he says. The first I ever heard him proclaim himself so.

"You'll do," I say. I should turn round and leave him be. But I'm an officer now.

"No," he says. "I'm *Handsome*. They make me work Oakland Plantation every day-dawn to dusk-dark. I'm damned. There is only one relief."

I dare not ask him what that is. I dunna belief in women's intuition, but now I fear Cat Harvey, on my life I do. I should push him off this mountain and run away.

"Kill me," he says.

"What?!" I say.

"Kill me. I need to be put down like a dog. I won't do it myself. Too much of a coward."

"Come back to camp, colonel," I say. I reach out my hand before he up and jumps off of the mountain.

"No!" he hisses, snatching his hand out of my grip. He unsheathes my revolver and slaps it in my hand. "*Kill* me, Irish," he says again. "We's a Shannon Scout. Do you know what that means? It means we did bad, bad things during the War. Wrongthings *you do not do*. We's beyond redemption. I might could bear Oakland in the morning if these nightmares I'm living would stop."

He raises my revolver up to his throat, the barrel beneath his chin. He willna let go of my hand, and I am too weak to yank it away, lest the gun go off.

"Do it," he whispers. I won't. "*Do it!*" he hisses. Again, I will not. Then quick as Satan, Cat Harvey snatches the gun out of my hand and now points it against my temple. "You Irish bitch!" he says. "On your knees."

I want to live; I should resist, but I do as I'm told.

He unsheathes his member from his jean pants and only then do I try to rise. But I hear the *snick* of my own revolver. Now it's cocked against my head. He forces his stiff member into my mouth and grabs hold of the top of my hair and rocks it back and forth. I should bite down on it, bite it off completely. But I want to live. *Lord Jaysus, don't let him pull that trigger.* He says very little. Cat Harvey says, "You see? You see?!" But I dunna understand. I only want to live. It takes a long time, but he eventually ejaculates. It is the first time I taste a man's seed. I gag on him. I nearly vomit.

But he lifts the revolver away from my head and then yanks me back to my feet. He slaps it again in my hand and says, "Now kill me!"

But I run. I think Cat Harvey will shoot me dead on that mountain. But I run anyway. I'm a banshee shrieking in the night, with the taste of his seed still on my tongue. Just when I'm about to run past the pickets, Darkish Llewellyn runs up to me. She carries a shotgun, which I take from her hands. I spin round and fire into the night.

But Cat Harvey is not there. Nothing was chasing me the entire time. I drop to my knees and my lower body collapses. I canna rise. And the taste of him still on my tongue. I grab at the dirt and proceed to eat it, eat it like Darkish Llewellyn standing beside me.

"No, Brianna," she says, trying to take the dirt from my mouth. But I eat it anyway. I always thought dirt was unclean. Now I know that it can cleanse.

WYATT THRAILKILL

Big commotion last night. Brianna O'Quinn ripped a shotgun blast into the night on Lookout Mountain. No one knows what she saw. She won't tell, neither. The widows on picket duty say they found her on her haunches, eating dirt. But they must of confused her with Darkish. No one else eats dirt but her.

I'm a man of few words. Back at LaGrange, my mama always told Gib and me, "Quiet, boys." I listened. Gib didn't.

But I want to ask Brianna what she seen last night. I want to do what I do best: listen. I sit with her at breakfast. But I don't know what to say. All the widows look at her queer. But I remain with her. Brianna's appetite has doubled since last night. She stuffs as much food in her mouth as possible. Eats like a hog, except she chews her food slow. She closes her eyes, which look like they might could tear up.

I want to talk to her, tell her whatever she thought she seen last night is gone. But I cain't. Don't have the words.

METTA DAHLGREN

W E CROSS THE Tennessee River for half the day since all the bridges had been fired during the War. It is solemn. At first, none of our widows talk to Brianna. We are ashamed that she scared us for no reason in the middle of the night. But though I had once found her too mannish for my liking, I ride up beside her on the march. I set the example for the rest of the widows. Brianna is our sister, after all.

"It is a lovely day," I say to her. She nods. I add, "We couldn't ask for better weather when crossing the river."

"No," she says. "'Tis a lovely day." But she says it in a way that leads me to believe she would rather it rain. Then Col. Cat rides past. He tips his hat to us. I acknowledge the greeting, but then I can feel the fury seethe from Brianna.

"What is it, dear?" I ask. "Is something the matter?"

She remains quiet.

"You know, you can tell me anything," I add. "Anything at all."

Brianna considers this, but then says, "When I finally speak truth, it will be from my gun."

It's frightening sometimes how much we hate Gen. Sherman. Brianna will make a fine warrior. All of the weak widows have fled our battalion, which may yet grow into a regiment once we leave Tennessee. Our hatred is empowering. I only hope and pray that Brianna's hatred won't get the best of her, like it did last night. We ladies have to keep cooler heads than gentlemen. It is what makes us more refined and deadly.

With all the trouble of overseeing our widows cross safely to the other side of the river, I have almost forgotten our Cause. It dawns on me that we are heading northwest, towards Nashville, not northeast towards Knoxville. But Sherman is *northeast*.

I ride up to the colonel immediately. Princess Ann plays her vagaries around Snaps, but I soon control her. "Col. Cat," I say.

"Miss Metta," he replies. His brute, Big Ugly, tips his hat to me.

"Are you aware that we are heading northwest?" I say.

"I am," Cat Harvey replies.

"Well, sir," I say. "How are we going to reach Ohio if we are traveling northwest?"

The colonel looks as though he is about to boil over in a rage. "Are you feeling mutinous today, lieutenant?" he asks. This is the first time he's called me by my rank.

"I was only saying…" I fall silent.

"You agree I fought in the War," he asks without asking.

"I… I don't understand."

"You agree I fought in Tennessee," he says.

"Yes, sir," I finally say.

"Then mebbe I know a little something about who all is loyal in this state and who airn't."

"I apologize," I say. "I didn't know."

"You widows want to be generals!" he says and throws up his hands. "Just like the Rangers! Nobody taking orders! Everbody out for their own glory!"

"Sir," I say. "We don't want glory. We want retribution."

"Then mind," he says, "we shall cross through Middle Tennessee. They's loyalty we shall find there. And mind, we shall recruit there, too. Press horses. Feed our growing army. All y'all widows want to be warriors. But you have to git to the battlefield first with the most. Or all is lost."

"I see."

"You see?" he says. "No, you do not. What's why you're gitting mutinous on me, Miss Metta. I don't want you to say another word to me till we git to Murphreesboro."

"What is in Murphreesboro?"

"My fucking wife and daughter, Metta."

I am shocked. I slap his face. Imagine, cussing in front of a lady.

But Cat Harvey backhands me across the face, and I fall off Princess Ann. Big Ugly is about to dismount to help me up, but the colonel holds him back.

I pull myself together. The widows are watching. I remount Princess Ann, only this time I throw my leg across the pommel. I'll not make the mistake of riding side-saddle again.

POLK INGRAHAM

We lost a monstrous lot of Georgia widows after Miss Brianna fired her shotgun at what she wouldn't say that night. A monstrous lot. Maybe three quarters crossed the Tennessee with us. The rest sneaked past our pickets in the middle of the night, I reckon. So my cousin give his *Special Order No. 10*: All captured deserters shall be hung from the neck till dead. It's a durn shame.

I tell my cousin, as we ride past Monteagle and turn west, "Will you really hang a lady?"

And he says, "You're such a shavetail Ingraham."

I might be shavetail, but I'm a proud Ingraham. I don't need to ride no horse to hold my head up high. So I say, "It's wrong! And you know it!"

"Polk," he says to me. "We's beyond good and evil now. This is *war*."

ELISHA TOOKE

WE RIDE UP some mountainous road and camp atop a plateau at a university name of Suwanee. It don't look like much. Yankees was here, and I reckon is why there ain't no menfolk to speak of now. My widows are on picket duty tonight, so we throw out our pickets and wait. We know Col. Cat will march right past them at some point in the night when his afflictions harry him. But we are under orders to halt any widow what tries to axcape. And I aim to follow them. I already lost five of my widows on the march. I told my widows I don't care if you do come from Sparta, I'll hang you myself.

The night is breezy. Is a full moon tonight. We hear something in the dark, and I say, "Halt! Who goes there?"

"Darkish Llewellyn," she says. It's that girl that eats dirt and talks to rocks. She has a passel of widows behind her.

"Turn back around," I say. "The colonel's orders."

But Darkish leads her widows past my pickets. I level my shotgun and the rest of my picket follows suit. I shout, "I warn you, Miss Darkish! My hand is steady and my aim is true! Turn back around now!"

But Darkish and her widows act like they don't hear me. They call my bluff. I signal my picket to lower their shotguns and remain put. Then I go after that queer gal, Darkish Llewellyn.

They lead me to a natural bridge, the first I ever seen. They walk cross it in the moonshine, though I cain't see how far a drop it is; it's still too dark. I won't set foot on it. I'm scared of heights. Darkish turns round and says to me, "This is a good rock."

"Awright, Darkish," I say. "The fun is over. Let's all turn back around before the colonel finds you gone."

Darkish then gits on her knees, like she's about to pray, and lowers her head till the left side of her face is flat on the surface of that natural bridge. It dawns on me that she's listening to the rock. The other widows stand in wait. One widow finally asks, "What's it say, Darkish?"

But Darkish don't answer. Instead, I say, "What kind of witchcraft is this?!" I don't believe in Heaven ever since I seen Hell run roughshod over Georgia. But I believe in the Devil. I reckon I cain't git shut of him.

By and by, Darkish raises her head along with the rest of her tiny body. She says, "This rock cries out for mercy, not justice. It told me we are in danger. That a handsome ghost haunts our colonel and won't let him go. That no woman is safe, not even our officers."

"Is it a demon?" one widow asks Darkish.

"No," Darkish replies. "But the ghost that haunts our colonel comes from Hell."

"What are we to do?" another widow asks. "He's our colonel!"

"This here rock didn't say," Darkish replies. "It only says we are in danger."

"Witchcraft!" I yell. "Don't listen to her! She's practicing witchcraft!"

But they act as if I ain't there. So I point my shotgun into the air and fire. It is the loudest sound I have ever heard. I nigh drop my gun.

"There he is!" a widow cries, and the rest scream. We see the silhouette of a man and think it's Col. Cat. But it's not. Turns out it's his cousin, Polk.

"Have you seen my cousin?" he asks. "Have you see Cat?"

No one answers him. Instead, Darkish leads the widows off of the natural bridge. So I arrest her on the spot. She ain't afeard of my shotgun. She ain't afeard of nothing. But she's still my prisoner. I won't have witchcraft practiced on my watch. I march her back to the picket line with Polk and the widows following.

But before I take her into camp, Darkish Llewellyn says to me, "The rock told me you're in the most danger, Elisha. It told me you're next."

CHARITY BELLE JONES

I HAVE LIVED IN Lincoln County all my years, right here in Tennsylvania. My father fought under the Revolutionary general after which our county was named, I'm proud to say. There was never any hate. When did this hate business appear? I don't know. I don't even use the word unless absolutely necessary.

I hate Col. Cat Harvey.

Because Tennsylvania showed its strong support for the Union, our town was spared much. Five of my boys and two of my grandbabies fought the Rebels in the War. They, too, were spared. God in His Providence spared them, and I thought this a most auspicious sign of the righteousness of the Union. I said as much whenever my sewing circle met to sew our soldiers more socks or long underwear. I told my girls, who are considerably younger than I, "we should look to Providence." After all, though some had lost their men, Tennsylvania had been spared.

Perhaps we made an idol of the Union. Perhaps we angered God with our idolatry, and so in His wrath He sent us a terrible Visitation in the form of Col. Harvey.

It began with the children. Our children began to play a game with a strange child. No one took notice of the boy, except that he carried a drum. The little drummer boy beat time, and our little children not only watched they began singing a strange song he had taught them. Of course, we thought the little drummer boy was an orphan. We waited for him to pass his butternut kepi around for us to place some coins in it. I was about to pass by on the sidewalk, on my way to our sewing circle, when the words of the chorus our children sang disturbed me. They sang:

> *You'll die, you'll die!*
> *By hundreds you will die!*
> *When Col. Cat rides his horse,*
> *By hundreds you will die!*

I stopped in my tracks and was about to admonish the children when suddenly a ragamuffin appeared with a box-fiddle. The drummer boy's father, perhaps. (We still thought Tennsylvania was safe, you see.) All our children clapped in time as the ragamuffin played rather sweetly for us all. Then he sang, too:

> *I never been to Pennsylvania*
> *But I hear that Tennsylvania's*
> *Twice as lovely in the summertime!*
> *You kin bet that Tennsylvania*
> *Is a heap better'n Themsylvania*
> *What say they ain't got food at suppertime!*

We clapped. We actually clapped for the ragamuffin and his little drummer boy, not knowing that a holocaust awaited us. Then he sang, along with our children:

> *You'll die, you'll die!*
> *By hundreds you will die!*
> *When Col. Cat rides his horse,*
> *By hundreds you will die!*

One of our menfolk pitched a dollar at the fiddler, and said, "Here! Play something else or go." And the fiddler stopped. He looked to the sky behind him. We did, too. We saw a cloud of dust just over our buildings. We thought (we actually thought in our ignorance) that it was the Union garrison we'd been promised. We clapped. We would be safe from any ruffians that would think twice before riding through Tennsylvania.

What fools we were.

I have lived to a ripe old age. If I were to die tomorrow, they would not look upon my death as a tragedy. But in all my years I have never seen anything as shocking as a band of widows riding in a column through our streets, wearing men's hats of every variety and armed to the teeth. No sooner had they appeared than the ragamuffin fiddler squawked out *The Yellow Rose of Texas*.

Our menfolk didn't know what to do. Some stood still. Others went inside the wooden buildings, perhaps to get their guns. (Why did our townfathers not build with brick? We would have been spared so much if only they had built with brick.) We ladies didn't know what to make of them. War widows, we assumed. But what were they doing riding through our town?

Then the boy colonel rode alongside the ranks on his bay charger, shouting orders to his widows. As soon as all of them were in town, he called for them to "halt!" And the music stopped.

Archibald Tyler, our sheriff, finally appeared from the crowd and said to the boy colonel, "Lookee here! What's the meaning of this? Clear off!"

Then Col. Cat Harvey slapped the leather on his left holster and shot him. He shot Archie Tyler! Our menfolk were about to raise their weapons when a retinue of widows raised theirs first. I could see a massacre on the horizon.

"Tennsylvania!" Cat Harvey said, just like any ordinary Southern boy would. But he was no longer a boy. You could see in his terrific eyes that there was nothing but hate in his heart. The hate only men are capable of. He said, "Tennsylvania, you get an *X*." And he drew a capital X in the air with his index finger that covered the entire town.

I spoke up. I couldn't help myself. I shouted, "Murderer!"

He turned to me, chuckled once, and said, "Ma'am. If you only knew."

I am in the habit of being taken seriously. So I shouted, "Look at what you did!"

"No," the boy colonel said. "Behold *my* family." And he outstretched his arms to show the widows behind him. "They grieve monstrously for their dead. Just like my wife did for me when I died. Tennsylvania, you shunned her. You kicked her and her family out of your town when she come down to refugee from Murphreesboro. You had no use for a Rebel gal."

Just then Andrew Fisher tried to draw his revolver, but a widow turned and fired her shotgun into his chest. Some of us screamed. I imagine I did, too. But Col. Cat Harvey merely nodded at the widow who fired her shotgun approvingly.

"Any more interruptions?" he asked. "Good. I'll be quick. This town aggrieves me. Smack in the middle of Rebel country, it cozied up to the Yankees. It watched from its perch as Georgia burnt. There is no pity in this town."

"Pity?!" I cried. "What know you of pity?!"

I expected to be shot dead on the streets of Tennsylvania. But I cared not a whit. Someone had to denounce Cat Harvey.

But he did not shoot me, nor did his mad widows. Instead, he considered me a moment until he said, "You're right. I know little of pity since 1865. I got the soldier's heart what druv up on me at Shiloh and won't give me peace. This town reminds me of my unpiteous heart. What's why it must burn."

Another man tried stopping him, Abe Tollison. But a widow drew her revolver on him the minute poor Abe raised his rifle, firing it up into the air.

"This town aggrieves me," Cat Harvey said, looking at the dead man. "I will take any man, woman or child what's loyal to the Confedricy." He waited. Then Mallory Duke picked up her child and walked into their ranks.

"Mallory Duke, how could you?!" I shouted. I never shouted until that wretched day.

She turned to all of Tennsylvania, her own people who'd not shunned her, even when her husband went off and joined the Rebels; she turned to us as if to say, "To Halifax with the lot of you!" and shooed us with her entire arm.

Then widows with pineknots in their hands appeared. And Col. Harvey raised a single match in his left hand. He struck it with his thumb and then lit a widow's pineknot. She then lit another and soon myriad pineknots smoked around them.

"Behold, Tennsylvania!" Cat Harvey shouted. "I bring fire from Georgia!" Then he turned and looked at me again with those hateful green eyes, and said, "You say there's no pity, ma'am. What I found is that them what airn't felt the pain theirselves must be *made* to feel it. Then they shall sympathize."

I fainted.

When I awakened there was nothing left of Tennsylvania except for ashes and what little brick with which we had built our town. So many of our men lay dead and hatless. So many of our ladies, now wailing widows.

Yes, we must have made an idol of our beloved Union, I think as I cross what once was Commerce Row onto Hamilton Street, where my home should be. I pass endless rows of brick chimneys until I reach my own. And what remains of my home? My home?! And where are my boys and grandbabies? Where are they?!

I cry out, "Edward…! John…! William…!" I cry out, "Robert…! Joseph…!" But no one will answer me. I cry out the names of my grandbabies, "George! Thomas!" (Why won't they answer me?!) "George…! Thomas…! Thomas…! Thomas…!"

SMIT HARVEY

I ADMIT I HAVE a passion for clubs, but not for this one. Not the Jolly Six, as they call themselves. They meet in a law office in Pulaski. Ex-soldiers, don't you know. And they've taken a shine to my little brother. Perhaps Catullus knows that it relieves their boredom to have had a bevy of armed widows ride through their town and then camp for the night. Perhaps he knows that they find him amusing. But after we burned down Tennsylvania and massacred its men, I have come to see that the baby of the Harvey family has not only grown up, he's grown brutal.

They pull pranks, this Jolly Six. Sophomore hijinks. They dress up in sheets and haze each other like fraternity brothers. And they love Greek, like fraternity brothers, too. One calls their club: *Kuklos*. I have studied my Greek. I know what it means.

I am a gambler, don't you know. But I do not understand the bet my little brother has made with these six. These six don't bet. They dare, like boys. When they saw that Catullus leads a column of armed widows, they howled with laughter on the front of their law office.

"Look at him," one of them said. "I bet he wears widow's weeds, too!"

Cat halted the column. He turned to the Jolly Six and said, "I bet I could still whip ass in a dress."

"I dare you to dress like a widow and then see what happens!" another of the six said. They laughed.

"I hear tell about some laughing assholes what wear bedsheets round this town," Cat said. "You wouldn't happen to know about them?"

They grew quiet then. One of the six said, "And suppose we did?"

"Well," Cat said. "I bet, come midnight, that I'll wear some widow's weeds, mount my horse and ride into the nigger camp yonder they call Freedmen's Town and won't nobody wearing their bedsheets will follow me."

"I bet they will," another of the six said. "I bet they will, too."

"We shall see," Cat said. But what is the wager? It is a bet of pride. A foul wager, don't you know.

It is fast approaching midnight, and we all of us wait for Catullus to emerge from his dog tent. He steps out of it completely shaven and wearing full mourning dress. The widows cry, "Whooooooo-hoo!" But the boys and I are ashamed for Cat. I hobble over to him, as if I walk on two good legs, before he mounts Snaps and makes a perfect fool of himself and my family.

"Catullus McGregor Harvey!" I say. "Halt right there!"

And he does. Cat turns to face me. I am furious.

"Have you no shame?!" I say. "You're a Harvey!"

But before I can beat him, my little brother laughs at me; he laughs at me. He says, "You're a fine one to talk, big brother. Whyn't you have a drink and settle down."

I throw a punch at him, but he ducks my blow, and my artificial leg comes loose and I fall legless. I reach for it, but Cat snatches it up and tosses it to Big Ugly.

"There," he tells him. "Don't give it back to him till I return."

"But why?" I practically yell. "What could this stunt possibly profit?"

My little brother mounts Snaps. He smooths out his black dress. Then he turns to me and says, "I'm gonna call them Kukluxers' bluff."

Then he puts spurs to Snaps and rides off for the edge of town.

One of the widows, Elisha or Eliza, I cannot tell which, says, "Now he's a widow, too."

DARKISH LLEWELLYN

The rocks cried me right out of my sleep. I took a piece of clay that I was saving and proceeded to eat it like I was starving. I could see it all: Col. Cat riding at the head of six laughing horsemen. Cat wears one of our widow's full mourning dresses. They wear white sheets to look like ghosts. Cat leads them to the edge of a Negro camp. At first, I think he draws his left gun to fire at the Negroes who have left their tents to see what rides their way. But instead, he fires a round into the air. I see the others fire into the air, too. They are laughing, but not Col. Cat. No. Cat rides Snaps hard. Both horse and rider are chomping at the bit, it seems.

That's all of this night that I see, but the rocks cry out again. They urge me to bear witness to what is to come. I see hundreds of them, maybe thousands of horsemen dressed in white sheets. They level their firearms and shoot into Negro homes. I see them hanging Negroes like so much fruit from the trees. The rocks will soak up their blood. It's too much, I see so much bloodshed, I try to make myself not see. But the rocks won't let me. Their dirt and clay is in my blood. Finally, I stop crying long enough to see it: Judgment Day itself. A burning crucifix without Christ there to save them.

HANDSOME

THE PLANTATION BELL sitting atop its wooden perch clangs out reveille for Oakland's reconcentration camps an hour before dawn, as always. I arise sweating from the nightmare of living as Cat Harvey. Our sins are multiplied whenever we conjoin, and I don't know how to stop haunting him the way he haunts me. Our Negro guards unlock our cabins, and it is time for roll call. They are spiteful men and women who remain in the twilight, I am told, because they turned on their own kind on the plantations.

They call my number: "*05031971!*" and I yell "Here, sir!" If I do not answer to my number, I am beaten. If I do not say *sir*, whether to a man or a woman, I am beaten. But I'm not a number. I am Henry Clay Somersett! I must always remember the name I had lost in the nightworld.

There is a stool pigeon in our midst. Our guards call out for number *01271972* to step forward. They search under his shuck mattress and find stolen food. He pleads not to be taken to the Box. But these Negroes had once told their former masters, like dutiful slaves, whenever they overheard plots hatching in the slave quarters; so they have no love for us: the former masters themselves.

I remember everything now, why I am in the reconcentration camp. My day always begins like this. First the plantation bell, then roll call, then the full memory of why I have been chosen for reconcentration on Oakland plantation.

What is worse than Hell? Purgatory.

I remember how I turned into a monster in the last year of the War.

How I, Henry Clay Somersett, did shoot and rape and burn to death those I called my enemies. All while intoxicated on liquor. All while calling myself a *scout*. I had burned with shame from time to time, but never enough to muster the moral courage to put a stop to the Scouts. Then, I would drink my liquor, and it would all happen again.

"Number *05031971!*" one of the guards says. "Eyes forward!"

I remember, too, what I had lost: my family. If I weep for them my guards will send me to the Box. So I force myself to wait. Day-dawn has not yet even broken.

Now we must walk Indian file out of the cabin. We are all starved for breakfast, despite knowing that we will be fed little than that which will keep our bodies alive. As we march to the "Pig's Trough," I also recall everything from the night before. My nightmares of Cat Harvey are more vivid and more real than the twilight itself. And as I march between *03301971* and 11081974, I know that Cat Harvey and I have relived our sins together.

We rode our horse in one of the widow's full mourning dresses. We led six horsemen wearing white sheets (like the Searchers in the nightworld) through a Negro camp. We raised hell. But even though not a soul was shot that night, we opened up something dark and terrible in those six.

"Remember this ride," we told the Kukluxers. And I'm afraid that they will.

VELLA MORTON

So now he wears a black dress. Just like the rest of us. He give a rousing speech in that dress he's taken to wearing, just before we lit out northeast for Marshall County. We lost some widows that night. They tried excaping, and our pickets shot them. They come from my command. Col. Cat made us hang the ones that was only wounded. Then he declared that he would hang anyone else that tries to excape. First time any of us had seen women hang from a tree. They looked like big black bells with their dresses ballooning in the breeze.

My sister don't like it. But I bet we don't lose none too many widows from now on.

But Marietta says, "It only takes one widow to burn Sherman's house."

I was glad Miss Bee Brewster warn't mixed up in this excaping business. Miss Bee is gentle, I can tell. Though when we burnt down Tennsylvania, she took the pineknot out my hand and lit a fire herself. Even though she's a lady, Miss Bee has the clear grit in her. I can tell. If it only takes one widow to burn Sherman's house, Miss Bee is it. All this unpleasantness. I know Bee has seen plenty. Why else crop your hair like a man?

Col. Cat rides up to Marietta and me. He bids us good morning and we do the same. I will never git used to seeing the colonel in a black dress. He says, "Morton sisters. We ride for Metropotamia, east of Lewisburg."

"What's thar?" I ax him.

"The town aggrieves me," he says. "Lot of Tories what helped us lose the War."

"Colonel," Marietta axes him, "you aim to wear that dress in Metropotamia?"

"Any man's free to take this off of me," the colonel says. "Like a steer, he can try."

POLK INGRAHAM

I'M A CAPTAIN now. All the Rangers are captains of the widows. So how come it that I still feel like a fifteen-year-old shavetail kid? After we burnt Metropotamia to the ground, we struck camp along Caney Spring. Cousin Cat has sent the widows to bathe theirselves. The Rangers remain in our dog tents, of course; but now I cain't help but think sinful thoughts. How many nekkid widows are in the spring right now? What all are they doing? Are they bathing each other, or just theirselves? What all do the widows look like without their black dresses? Makes my pecker stiff in my jean pants.

Wonder what Darkish Llewellyn looks like without her dress.

I cain't take it! I wish the widows'd hurry up and bathe. If I were alone in this dog tent, I might could do something about it. But the captains are my messmates. Gibby Thrailkill tries to take a peek through the flap, but it's no use. Besides, he's only got one hand.

But I got two. One could hold open the flap of this dog tent just enough so I could see the bathing widows in the spring. The other could grasp my stiff pecker and stroke it. I bet Darkish Llewellyn is bathing right now. Bet she looks like a faun in that spring water.

I cain't take it! I just cain't take it!

JOHN HENRY HOLIDAY

A NEST OF BUSHWHACKERS killed two of our widows and wounded one on the Lewisburg Road. They shot up a few of our horses mighty bad, too. Without waiting for an order, Uncle Calsas jumps off the wagon and commences tending to the horses, while Col. Cat dives into the thicket where the gunsmoke gives the bushwhackers away. No one is tending to the wounded widow, Mrs. Marietta Morton, so I jump off the wagon and look after her arm. I like to tear off my shirt and then wrap it around the wound and tie it tight. She doesn't howl. She just looks at me with eyes clear as day.

Col. Cat emerges from the bushes with a ragged bushwhacker. His revolver is pointed at his head. Mrs. Marietta rises and grabs her shotgun, but the colonel orders her to "Halt right there! Hold your fire, Marietta!" She grunts and drops the shotgun to her side.

"Awright, Bushie," he says to the bushwhacker, then cocks his revolver. "Where all is your hideout?"

"I live *here*, you queer!" the bushwhacker says.

Col. Cat shoots and spills the bushwhacker's brains onto the nearest bush. Then he inspects Mrs. Marietta's arm. He unties my shirt and checks the wound.

"That arm has to come off," he declares.

Marietta snatches it away and raises her shotgun at his chest. She says, "Like a steer, you can try!" Then she calls for her sister, Mrs. Vella.

May rosined lightning strike me down dead if I didn't see Vella Morton fly down on her from her horse and knock her sister out with the butt of her shotgun.

"Do it!" Vella tells Col. Cat with tears in her eyes. "Make it quick! We got bushwhackers to catch!"

Four widows pick up Mrs. Marietta just as one of the wounded horses keels over, dead.

"Calsas," Col. Cat says. "Calsas!" he yells.

But Uncle Calsas stands stock still, staring at the dead horse. Tears fill up his bloodshotted wall-eyes. Yet before the colonel says his name again, Uncle Calsas saunters over to the wagon and fetches him a bonesaw.

"Come on, Little Doc," he tells me. "You'se gonna hold her arm out straight."

GEORGE WASHINGTON SHUTE

HE ASKS IF I have any last words. The queer boy in the widow's dress. He already hung the rest of us. All my male relations. Why he's saved me for last, I don't rightly know. Maybe cause he thinks I'm the leader, like him.

I wear a sign round my neck that declares: "*Death to All Bushwhackers.*" I reckon I won't git proper buried. I reckon my soul will hang in the tree with me for eternity. But at least I'll die knowing that the Union is preserved. At least I'll die with my own sons and nephews.

When he strung up my boy, James, two hulking widows forced me to watch. The boy in widow's weeds slapped the horse, and James Madison dropped down. He kicked and he kicked for life. And I was forced to watch him die. After that first sight, the rest was easy. I watched Thomas, Andrew, Monroe and Knox all drop the same way.

Then he has the nerve to ask me do I have any last words.

I look him in the eye and tell him, "No."

JINCY McBRIDE

Some widows come west from the Mountain, and Cat Harvey give them to me.

"You speak their language," he tells me. "You go talk mountain-talk to them."

"Just you wait till we find a preacherman," I say. But I know that no preacherman'd ever marry me proper to a man in a dress.

"Cain't you see I'm in mourning," Cat says and displays hisself in his widow's weeds.

For ever three widows we gain, thar's two widows that flee us in the night. Most git away, but some don't. They git hung by the roadside.

Cat Harvey drinks his Devil's Brew now raggler. He don't git purely rosined when he drinks it. He come alive. He plots Gen. Sherman's total ruination with the lieutenant widows then. I heered him speak it.

I cain't wait any longer, I'm so boiling mad. Like a horse that has the evil foot I cain't walk ten steps without thinking bout it. I rise up from my bedroll and sneak over to Cat Harvey's dog tent. I think I am going to kill him. I got my knife on me. When I kill him I know the widows will gang up on me. I know a big ruction will ensue and I'll be hanged. But I don't care. Cat Harvey married me like a bear. And he thinks he kin git away with it?!

No one guards his tent, not even Big Ugly. So I sneak in it and find him asleep. I think I'm about to plunge my knife in his guts, but I draw the blade under his chin and wake the bastard up instead. I could slit his throat any second. All he has to do is move.

"Do it," Cat finally says. "I got no heart left but the soldier's heart. Do it, Jincy."

I don't know what come over me, I git mad. I want to slit his throat and hear him squeal like a winter hog. But instead I press the knife gainst his throat and reach under his dress for his manhood. He darest not move. Cat Harvey looks me in the eye with them green eyes of his. Surprised, I see they's resigned. I could unmarry us with one stroke of the blade. Then force him to look at his own manhood bleeding in my hand. But I don't do it. I want him to suffer the way I did back when he married me in North Caroliner. So I yank his manhood till it stiffens. I let go. I keep the blade firm gainst his throat. Then I raise up my dress and straddle Cat Harvey. I guide his manhood into my womanhood. And then I commence erasing the deed. I erase his manhood with my womanhood. He tries to buck, but I press the knife gainst his throat.

"Don't you holler!" I hiss, just like a wildcat and whisper in his ear, "*I'll show you. I'll show you.*"

BEE BREWSTER

"I KNOW WHY the widows bolt," Darkish Llewellyn tells me on the march to Chapel Hill. I don't like this clay-eater. She scares me. It seems that she always appears when you least expect her. Does she want me to ask her why? Why some of our widows flee him? Why they risk hanging to flee Cat Harvey?

She knows I know the reason why.

"Leave me alone," I tell her. "Go eat your clay."

Then Vella Morton rides alongside us and shoos Darkish away. She has been promoted captain. The first widow so honored. She earned her promotion for knocking out her sister so Uncle Calsas could saw off Marietta's arm. They haven't spoken to each other since.

"Are you awright, Miss Bee?" Vella asks. I know Capt. Vella has taken me under her wing. I'm afraid I know the reason why. She has feelings for me, feelings I cannot return to her. I want to show her how much I care about her, but somehow her feelings seem to get in the way.

"I will be fine," I tell my captain.

WORTH SOMERSETT

HE DRINKS HIS *Vin Mariani* in his black dress and don't even count the gold. I'm a major now, second in command of these women. But I care not a damn about William T. Sherman. Soon as I avenge Scip, I'm lighting out and taking my share of the gold. Cat Harvey can go to hell.

He drinks his *Vin Mariani* in his black dress and watches as more widows from Shelbyville flock to our ranks. And the war orphans! More mouths to feed. More horses for Uncle Calsas and Little Doc to shoe.

He pays us in pesos, when he knows I want gold eagles. If he paid me in eagles, I could buy something useful like a Kentucky thoroughbred. As it stands, our money stays within the circle of the regiment. We exchange it with each other, not with the world outside.

But he drinks his wine in those widow's weeds and calls his councils of war. I know that Gibby Thrailkill would light out with the money, if I plotted with him. He'd do it, too. He guards the war chest every chance he gets. We could guard it together and then light out in the middle of the night. Divide it up equal and go our separate ways.

I give it to Cat, though. He rode into Shelbyville by himself in that dress and come out the other side of town with a bevy of widows.

"What'd you say to them?" I asked.

"Nothing," he said. "I told their men not one of them could make me take off this black dress. And when none of them did, their womenfolk took to their horses and mules and followed me. Call me a *real* man."

So real men wear dresses in 1865. The world has turnt upside down and over.

CORNELIUS COGDELL DUDLEY

My STARS. AND to think it couldn't get any worse! It could be the greatest show on earth! If only we weren't stranded on the God forsaken Shelbyville pike in God forsaken Middle Tennessee. I have myself to blame. We were en route for Atlanta, where I knew the garrison would pay top dollar to see my circus and menagerie. But I had to turn my circus onto the Shelbyville pike when we left Murphreesboro. I heard there was a pair of Siamese twins that lived somewhere on the pike. That they even fought for the Rebels! My circus has everything under the sun: a strong man, a bearded lady, a wolf boy, lithe jugglers, clowns of every shape and size! But to possess a pair of Siamese twins! Everyone would flock to see *C.C. Dudley's Amazing Circus and Menagerie* then!

But my stars. It was one disaster after another—arguments, escaped tigers, wheels getting stuck in the mud—my caravan came to a grinding halt. And do you think I found my Siamese twins? Oh I found twins, all right— two perfectly *normal* twins. I am more conjoined to the bearded lady when she lets me congress with her for an extra two dollars! No, these twins... and now my circus faces utter ruination.

Why did Cat Harvey cross my path?! Why did he and his wicked band of widows ever ride north on the pike? Why did the gods see fit to punish me, C.C. Dudley, and for what crimes?! Because I cheat the public a little? My public gets the greatest show on earth! They demand that I cheat them a little! It is an unspoken agreement that we have always had!

He took my elephant: Goliath. Cat Harvey just walked right up and took him. "Pressing horses," he called it.

I must laugh to keep from crying. Normally, we have to turn kids away from joining our circus. At least the ones that show no talent. But here I stand, C.C. Dudley, ringmaster, and my stars, would you believe that half of my circus left with my elephant! Who has ever heard of a circus freak *leaving* the circus to join an even greater freak show, I ask you. Who indeed! Seven of my clowns tumbled after the procession of wild widows on horseback. Two of my best jugglers juggled every pistol, shotgun and rifle these widows gave them, and followed. My strong man challenged some creature called Big Ugly to a fight, and Big Ugly whipped him. (He has lost all self-esteem!) My beloved bearded lady shaved off her beard and put on a widow's dress. Lion-tamers, ropewalkers, trapeze artists—gone!

All Cat Harvey did was walk up to Goliath and take him, dressed in a widow's black dress. Now I am ruined! Utterly ruined!

Ah me, poor me! What use have I with the rest of this circus?!

UNCLE CALSAS

HIS HUCKLEBERRY IS beyond my persimmon.

SMIT HARVEY

My LITTLE BROTHER. He wears clown makeup now. In that black dress Catullus looks like a perfect minstrel in a show. I protest. I put my foot down. But I am merely another captain for him to order from the perch of his elephant.

"Yes, but think of your name!" I say. "Think of our family name!"

"My name is Galveston now," he tells me in front of everyone. "I am an island. I am a rodeo clown."

ETHAN BRIARSTONE

I AM HIS GUEST.

By the time I had reached Murphreesboro with my fellow travelers ("speculators" he would call them) I had already heard the rumors in the streets of Nashville. I was looking for a story to file with my paper, the *New York Herald*, and instead the story found me. We had only just assembled with a contingent of troopers, destined for Atlanta. The rumors of Cat Harvey and his band of angry widows was mere myth meant to scare us. They sounded like children's ghost stories do to adults. I was more afraid of bushwhackers and highwaymen. It was the only reason I joined the party of entrepreneurs, timber barons, who were interested in Georgia pine. The timber barons hated me once they found out I was Unitarian. The troopers hated me when they found out I was a pacifist. But I worked for the paper. They needed me as much as I did them.

We had hardly left Murphreesboro when I noticed how birds began scattering from the trees, and rabbits began crossing our path. The troopers drew their rifles and told us, "Wait right here." Then they left us on the roadside. Soon, we heard the crack of gunfire, and every man grew alert then. The timber barons drew their revolvers. I had nothing but my pencil. They sneered at me and we waited.

One doesn't expect to see an elephant the size of Goliath tramping on the turnpike in the middle of Tennessee. But there to our astonishment was Cat Harvey, dressed like a widow in full clown makeup, riding Goliath. He startled our horses. They played their vagaries with us so much that no one could draw a sight on Harvey. No sooner had we got control of them then we were surrounded by widows with pointed guns.

The timber barons threw down their revolvers instantly. I wished I had the courage to take out my journal and write it all down right there while it was happening. But I thought I faced my death. I began to pray silently to the only God I knew.

Cat Harvey climbed down from his elephant, but did not address us. Instead, he searched through our saddlebags.

"Well, well," he told the barons. He pulled some papers out and began reading them. "Speculators," he finally declared.

"Now see here!" one of the barons said. "Those are my God damn papers!"

Cat Harvey dropped them and we watched them fall to the ground. He looked at us as if to say, "Oops." Then he began laughing. It was the wickedest laugh I have ever heard.

"Don't s'pose you old boys knew 'bout these woods," Harvey said. He twirled once like a little girl, then said, "All these woods are *mine*. You cain't have them."

"Listen," one of the barons said. "I'm worth a lot of money to you. If you just tell us your ransom—" but Cat Harvey shot him dead.

I was frightened out of my wits—I'd never been so afraid.

"Timber!" he cried at the lifeless body. Nobody laughed.

"Please, mister, mister…" another baron said.

"My name is Galveston," Harvey said. "I am the Rodeo Clown."

"Mr. Galveston," the baron said. But he was hushed by the third. Cat Harvey shot *him* dead.

Now there was only one baron left.

"So you thought you'd take my Southern pine away," Harvey said.

"Mr. Galveston," the baron said. "Come, let us reason together."

And just like the others, Harvey shot him dead. I prepared my soul for the Hereafter.

"You," Harvey said to me. "You don't carry a gun. How come?"

I knew I was dead anyway, so I told him: "Cowards carry guns."

Cat Harvey's face broadened into a smile. It was only then that I saw Galveston the Rodeo Clown.

"Takes a lot of sand to call a man coward without a gun in your hand," Harvey told me. I had nothing more to say. I awaited my death. "I reckon you airn't part of this party of speculators."

"I'm a journalist," I told him.

"I see," he said. "Another Wordsworth. Well, Wordsworth, I welcome you to the South. Please partake of my hospitality."

Now I am his "guest." I dare not leave.

CUFF

L ASSY ME, I sure do miss me some Doll baby. Massa Cat say she and Miss Lorie is in Murpheyboro. What's why he send me into town all by myself. I can pass a picket guard easy. All I has to do is act natural-like. Smile for the whitefolks till they smile back. Massa know I can fool them, axspecially Yankees. A Yankee'll might ax you bout where all to find hid gold, is all.

I miss my Dolly, I loves me some Doll baby. She the sweetest gal I know. (She a lady, too.) I court her during the War. She act all airy with me at first. Take me for a field hand cause I come from Texas. But I know soon as I see her that I make Doll my wife. She act all biggity and airy, just cause she Miss Lorie's pet, but I know she sweet on ole Cuff. I can tell. What's why I make her laugh with my pranks. Naw, she sweet on me. I can tell. What's why we git married, like we do. What's why she birth me a fine boy, like she do.

I come to pass the picket guard and what do I find but a nigga picket in the moonshine. They ax me all sorts of questions a white picket won't ax.

"Is you a deserter?" they ax me. Like I's been a Yankee and wear the blue.

"How you gonna call me a deserter?" I say. "I come to jine up."

Then they ax me where all I axcape from. I tell them I axcape from McMinnyville. I tell them a whole heap of lies and they let me pass.

Massa say I's a good liar, and it true. I lie to him, I hates to admit. Some time he catch Cuff in a lie, some time he don't. Some time he beat poor Cuff when he not sure. Some time he take pity on Cuff cause we born the same year and know each other all our natural lives on Magenta plantation. But I loves Massa Cat, I do. I just loves my Dolly and the little baby more. What's why I run away that time when Columbia's set to burn. I run away to find them.

I ain't never find them.

But that all in the past. I know the streets of Murpheyboro sure as I know my own hand. Soon I git to see my Doll baby. Soon I git to look at my baby boy what look like he daddy, too. I pass through the square easy (a nigga is invisible in a war). I pass through the square and see that it a nigga garrison here. I raised to believe I hates the Yankee blue. But when I ax myself, Cuff, ain't dat a fine uniform? I hates to admit that I say "yep." A nigga with a gun is a mighty sight to see. I like to jine up, if I didn't loves Massa so. If I didn't loves my Doll baby and my boy.

He name Virgil. I name the little chap that cause Massa Virgil die in the War (Massa Cat don't know it but he my brother, too. We all three Harvey brothers).

I turn the corner on Main Street (I can read when I wants to. When I got a good reason, I can read). I walk in the moonshine till I reach Vander-peek House.

I like to cry. I's just twenty steps away from seeing my Doll baby and baby boy!

FRANK VANDERPEEK

THERE IS A knock at my back door. At this hour? I pick up my musket and I tell Nero, my nigger man, to answer the door. Murfreesborough is garrisoned, this time with nigger troops, so I expect to see anything when Nero opens the door.

It is Cuff, my son-in-law's body servant.

"Well don't just stand there, boy!" I declare, relieved. "Come in! Quickly now!" And he does. I'm so happy to see him that I nearly cry. I have not heard news of my daughter nor my grandchild since they fled Atlanta. That was six months ago. I have heard nothing but rumors ever since. Now that Cuff is here… I practically embrace the boy, I'm so overjoyed. "Out with it!" I say. "What news of Miss Lorelei? Where is my daughter, Cuff?"

Cuff looks at me confused. "Mr. Frank," he finally says. "I come to fetch Miss Lorie for Massa Cat…"

"But she is with him, is she not?" I say. "Answer me!"

"No, sir. No, sir," he says. Then he begins to cry.

"Where is your master?" I demand. "Where is Cat Harvey?"

Cuff hesitates to tell me. He looks sidelong at me. Then he says, "Massa gonna feel mighty poorly than he already is Mr. Frank when I tell him Miss Lorie and the baby ain't here."

I could beat this nigger within an inch of his life for not answering me. "Not here?!" I roar. "Of course they're not here! They fled south to look for your master! They fled south to remain under *his* protection!"

Cuff proceeds to cry and moan. He asks me, weakly, "And Doll not come home neither?"

I drop my musket and fly at him in a rage. I beat Cat's nigger with my own two hands. He howls and he begs for me to stop. But he had the audacity to ask about Lorelei's maidservant when my Lorie is still gone missing. I don't care if he chapped a child with Doll. My Lorie has gone missing.

"Of course Doll's missing!" I tell him when my rage subsides. "She's with Miss Lorelei, isn't she?"

Cuff drops to the ground like a sack of meal. He sits Indian style on my floor, crestfallen.

"Up!" I say. I kick his folded leg with the side of my foot. "Up, nigger! I won't have this! You have to return to your master, immediately. You must tell your master I demand to see him. Tell him his father-in-law demands he come at once!"

I signal for Nero to pick Cuff up. I won't stand for this display. Not while my Lorie and granddaughter is gone missing. Nero lifts him up with some effort. When Cuff stands alone he looks like the ghost of himself.

"Out, Cuff!" I say. "Out of my house and back to your master. Hurry!"

He does not move. The nigger has the temerity to remain standing in my house. I feel another rage boiling inside of me but know that another thrashing will not speed him. I expect him to cry once more, but Cuff does not. Instead, he looks me in the eye. (Imagine, a nigger looking at me, Frank Vanderpeek, in the eye!) and says, "Why."

"Why?" I say. "Why?!" If I had my musket in my hand I would have shot him on the spot.

"Why," Cuff says. "They dead and gone now."

ELISHA TOOKE

S<small>HE WAS RIGHT.</small> That witch Darkish Llewellyn was right. I was next.

The colonel just found out that his wife and daughter was dead, like as not. Leastways they never returned to Murfreesborough, like they's s'posed to do. Col. Cat was aggrieved in his sorrow. My Spartan widows had already took to talking about his sanity. Why else would he wear full mourning dress? Why else would he wear clown makeup now, like a fool? But I had questions that he wouldn't answer proper. Why did we avoid Murfreesborough when there was still a niggra garrison thar? How did he aim to feed these circus freaks that follow us like wagon-dogs? How did he aim to feed his elephant?

"Ugh," he said on the night that it happened. Just like a perfect Indian would.

I can just hear Mama telling me, "Why didn't you leave him alone, Elisha? Why didn't you let the man grieve in peace?" I can just hear Mama's husky voice telling me I should have stayed in camp. I should have never crossed those pickets to follow the colonel in that state that he was in. I can just hear Mama telling me a man that just lost his wife and daughter is a dangerous animal. She would ask me why I followed such a man carrying a gun and a bottle of wine in the first place? And all I could say in my defense is that I had questions that he wouldn't answer proper.

But did you have to ask, did you have to come out and ask Cat Harvey, Elisha, why he hung so many of us widows these days?

"They displeased me," he said, then drank a draught of that *Vin Mariani*, that crazy wine that we should ban altogether.

I can just hear Mama's voice. Telling me I should have left the man alone. Scolding me for letting him do what he did to me. Just like Darkish Llewellyn said.

Some things you must put out of your mind. You shut the door and lock it and pray that it won't come in some other way.

"It didn't happen," I tell myself on the march. I tell myself it couldn't of happened. Cause how could it when all I did was ask a simple question? I tell myself it was just a nightmare I had about a clown in a black dress, is all. Just a nightmare.

But I can hear Mama saying, "If it was a nightmare, then why do you still wash yourself every chance you git?"

JOHN HENRY HOLIDAY

H<small>E TELLS ME</small> on the Nashville Pike, "Little Doc, go fetch me some pliers from Uncle Calsas."

The colonel has been in a bad way ever since he learnt that his wife and daughter never come home from the War. Probably dead. We got a whole bevy of Murphreesborough widows that follow us from the south and Smyna widows that rode up to meet us from the north. Some still come down from the Mountain. Big widows with man-sized hands. Some of them want to form a democracy in camp. But the colonel declared, "I am Galveston, the Rodeo Clown! I *am* your democracy!"

I fetch the pliers from Uncle Calsas, like I'm told. Then I return to Col. Cat's dog tent. The colonel is in a bad way. I'd try to run away if I didn't think he would hang me.

"Little Doc," he calls me. He sits on a log that the widows always tote on the march. "I am in pain," he says. "There is a star of pain glowing bright in my mouth. I need you to take those pliers in your small hand and fix it."

"What?" I say. I'm no dentist. I'm still just a boy.

"Take those pliers and grab hold of the sorry tooth what aggrieves me."

I hesitate, which is not a good thing to do in Cat Harvey's regiment. I say, "Don't you want to drink some of your wine first?" I know how it give him comfort.

"No," he says. "My wife and daughter's slaughtered somewheres. I want to feel something other than the pain."

He points to the tooth that ails him. I take a breath and then go to work in the colonel's mouth. He doesn't struggle as I work that tooth out with my pliers. I yank it good, but it won't budge. I half expect Col. Cat to chomp off my fingers, I'm yanking so hard. Then I grab hold of the pliers with both hands and give it one last good yank that sets it free. I hear the tooth crack out of Col. Cat's mouth. Only then does he howl in pain. Tears well up in his eyes. They streak the white grease paint down his face. Blood fills up his mouth and stains it redder than it already is.

Is he gonna kill me? I drop the pliers onto the ground. But no, Cat Harvey turns to the side and spits out the rest of his bloody pieces of tooth. And he laughs. He laughs bloody. He is Galveston, the Rodeo Clown indeed.

"Doc Holiday," he calls me, laughing. He picks up the pliers, opens and closes them once, and says, "Wrong tooth."

I run out of the tent before the colonel reaches into his mouth with those pliers and grabs hold of the right one.

METTA DAHLGREN

It has been a month since we left Savannah, and we have already traveled five hundred miles. Now we march on Nashville. Widows flock to us by the dozens. They come from every knob, hill and creek. They have heard of our crusade to burn Sherman's home to ashes and are spoiling for a fight. Soon, we truly shall be the Widows' brigade, despite our still losing widows in the middle of the night. My Swainsboro widows have become officers, and I am now captain. We no longer ride side-saddle, not since Col. Cat reprimanded me. (I shall not lie. I thought about fleeing camp that night. No gentleman hits a lady. But this is war.) So now we ride like men. I must admit it is the most natural way to ride horses. But we are still ladies. We don't wear slouch hats; my girls wear fashionable Moabs on the march. A girl must remind herself of the finer things, even in 1865.

But it has been a month now. We are camped outside of La Vergne. I don't know why we expected to leave our Monthly Visitor behind in Georgia. We need rags, and soon, to catch our monthly flow. It seems our cycles have grown in synch with one another, a good sign. But now I must tell the colonel that we are in need. It is the most indelicate conversation I shall have with a man, especially one who wears full mourning dress and makeup.

"Capt. Dahlgren," he says. "What's that on your head?"

"It's a Moab," I say. "Do you like it?"

"It looks like a warshpot."

"Well I'm sure men can't be expected to know the latest fashions," I reply. "But I am not here to speak of fashion. I'm here on a most indelicate matter."

He throws up his hands. The colonel says, "Don't tell me your women's on the rag, too!"

"*Colonel!*" I say. I am shocked beyond belief. I feel my entire throat and face turning beet red. In another life, I would have marched out of his tent and rode Princess Ann away from shame.

"All my widows is taken to bleeding," he says. "Brianna's, Eliza's, Elisha's, the Morton sisters'... all y'all's worse than my seven Harvey sisters when they git together for too long. The entire camp smells of blood and scares my elephant."

"*Colonel!*" I say. "Remember you are in the presence of a lady!"

"I'm in the presence of an officer what wants me to combat Nature."

I regain myself. I am, after all, a captain now. I look Cat Harvey in his green eyes and ask, "How do you expect us to march on Nashville, if we are in such a state?"

"I already thought on this," he says. "Assemble your widows an hour fore dawn breaks."

"Yes sir," I say. "What shall I tell my girls?"

"You tell them that tomorrah they's gonna pick cotton. Enough cotton for their cooters and some more to stop up my ears."

ETHAN BRIARSTONE

IT HAS BEEN days since my captivity, and I am already given a task in Cat Harvey's doomed army of widows, orphans and circus freaks.

"Wordsworth," he says. He dismisses the two huge mountain women who guard me. He takes a seat beside me on a log. "Break out your pencil and git your words' worth."

I have decided that, though I am Cat Harvey's "guest," I am a journalist first. So I decide to oblige my captor.

"Write this down," he says. "*Good people of Nashville. I am Galveston, the Rodeo Clown. You might could have heard I dress like a widow and wear makeup, but like Alexander the Great, I ride into battle on a elephant. I hear tell that Andy Johnson has issued a proclamation what give amnesty and pardon to any man willing to take the oath. It aggrieves me. I will never swaller the dog and become a galvanized Yankee. Nashville has been garrisoned since my brother Virgil died of pneumonia. He would of lived if the Yankees hadn't-a forced us to evacuate the city. They made my wife and daughters refugees in their own country. And now they are dead. They are dead, and I am a orphaned widow. Death has held High Carnival over the land. The world is a circus and I am its greatest freak. But this circus is also a rodeo and I am its supreme clown. I am calling on all the lost, orphaned widows to take up arms gainst your captors. To rise up! and jine my cavalry. We don't come as liberators. We come as* Regulators."

Cat Harvey is about to leave when I ask, "May I interview you?"

He turns round and smiles eerily at me. "You are my guest," he says. "Of course you can."

My words may never see the pages of the *New York Herald*, but I will be damned if I remain a prisoner without having something to show for it.

What do you ask a man like Cat Harvey? I begin with the obvious. "Why do you wear a widow's dress?"

"Cause I'm in mourning," he says. I almost forget to write this down.

"Whom do you mourn?" I ask. "Your wife and daughter?"

"Yes, Lorelei and Amelia. I mourn them both. But I took to wearing the widow's weeds long before I found out they was dead."

"Then who else do you mourn? Your brother, Virgil was his name?"

"It still is," Cat says. "Yes, I mourn poor Virgil. We was Irish twins, and he were the older one. I took to wearing his clothes after he died in Murfreesborough. I didn't snap out of it till Shiloh."

"The battle of Shiloh?" I ask. "Were you there?"

He considers me a moment, then says, "Cat Harvey were there. He died on the first day. Shell exploded under his sergeant's horse and it scattered their remains on him. I thought I were still alive. That God in His Providence had saved me. But now I know that I indeed died that day. Now I'm the hungry ghost what haunts his body."

"Galveston," I say.

"I am the island conquistadors could not conquer."

I write this down, too. I ask Cat Harvey, "What do you want?" This confuses him. So I ask, "What do you hope to gain?"

"What do I want?" he repeats. "I want to light a fire in the North what them that lit the fires in the South have not yet seen. I want to find Northrop's Scouts, one-by-one, and make their wives widows, like me."

"Who are Northrop's Scouts?" I ask.

"You've heard of Kilpatrick?" he asks. I nod. "Then you know he rode cross Georgia and the Caroliners with Tecumseh Sherman. Capt. Northrop was chief of Kil's scouts. You know what a scout is, don't ya?" I nod. But he says, "No, you do not. *I* were a scout. And a scout in this war is a nasty thing. He goes off on his own hook and commits acts of depredation at will."

"And you were a scout," I say.

"One of Shannon's Scouts," he says without pride or shame.

"Who were these scouts? These Shannon's Scouts?"

"Let's just stick to your questions," he says.

But I persist. "Who was Capt. Shannon? Where did you scout? What was your mission?"

Cat Harvey rises from his log. "Interview's over," he says. "As my guest you should know that it is impolite to ask me about the Scouts. It aggrieves me. But I am your host. You are free to move about this camp."

"Am I free to move beyond it?" I ask.

"Naturally," he says, but then adds, "My widows on picket duty won't shoot an unarmed man, I reckon."

Then he proceeds to leave me.

"Col. Harvey," I say. "Galveston!" Only then does Cat Harvey turn round. I hold up his missive to Nashville. "You have forgotten your letter."

"No, I have not, Wordsworth," he says. "Give it some of that Yankee flourish. Then take it to Marietta Morton."

"How shall I know which one is she?" I ask. There are hundreds of widows in camp, perhaps a thousand.

"She's my courier," Cat says. "The Morton sister with only one arm left."

DARKISH LLEWELLYN

NASHVILLE IS A rock, the past fossiled in the memory of its stone. It tells me the future embedded in the living rock. I cannot sleep. I dare not sleep. Cat Harvey will send for me. Maybe tonight, maybe tomorrow, maybe next month. I will go to him, knowing that he has been cursed with his afflictions. I will go to him because he is afflicted.

We are all fossils of the War. Sherman didn't brush the land with fire; he washed it with floodwater, and we sunk into the bloodstained earth, and there we struck our outraged poses until we were fossiled. But this rock is too loud. It screams at me till I cry. It tells me why the widows flee in the middle of the night. It tells me who is next. "Leave me alone!" I cry into the night. Then I eat my clay. It only makes it worse. The Nashville dirt is in my teeny body that will never be big enough to fight off Cat Harvey when he sends for me. It tells me who is next. It does not say her name, but I know that Metta Dahlgren is in danger.

MADAME LASHVILLE

In my business you meet all sorts. This one fancies you tickle him, that one fancies the lash. They all want to be punished. So I punish them.

When the Yankees came in '62, I thought, 'Well, Lashy, there goes business.' I had misconceptions about Yankees, you see. Give me a big strapping Southern boy, and I'll give him a right smart spanking while I make him suck his own thumb. It all goes back to their mothers, I have come to believe. They all want Mama. A Southern boy is never too old to punish. But I found that the Yankees—Hoosiers, Buckeyes, Huskers, too—loved my services just as much as any boy in butternut or gray. Business thrived. I could finally afford that house on the hill I always wanted. I live a quiet life by day. No one in Nashville suspects a thing (or dares suspect it).

You meet all sorts, like I said. But it takes a special sort of customer to request Dolly Mop and the Angry Nanny. It involves the Leather Maiden, for one. I feel obligated to warn my customers away from it, especially first-timers. Most boys balk at the last minute. They order something else. Only a special few go through with our performance.

You meet all sorts, but when Mr. Galveston drove the Yankee pickets in with tales of wild widows and elephants, setting off a general panic; I somehow knew that we would need to oil the Leather Maiden. I ordered the house cleaned from top to bottom, and I put on my finest stockings and waited to receive him.

We watched from our window as Mr. Galveston's widows drove the garrison out of the city. The cowards. I was not a bit surprised; after all, I had given half of their officers the lash.

By evening, he somehow found me. So I knew he must have been to Nashville before. I am not so easily found. But he found me. And I laid eyes on him for the first time. His full mourning dress did nothing to faze me. (Had I not forced hundreds of men to wear dresses and demand they call themselves "my wench"?) It wasn't even his clown makeup; although, truth be told, I have always been afraid of clowns. They never made me laugh, even as a girl. And Mr. Galveston's clown makeup was so hastily painted on, as if he wasn't living amongst hundreds of women who could properly paint his face. No, it was his eyes, his crowsfooted eyes the color of limes. I knew the violence in those eyes, ten times worse than anything I had been paid to commit.

Now it is night. He asks, "What is the most painful?"

I steer him away to other choices on our menu, but I know he won't be dissuaded.

"You're holding back," he says. "I can tell."

"It's expensive," I finally say. I am afraid of what he will do to me if I play the Angry Nanny.

"Money is no object," he says. "I have gold enough."

I name an outrageous price. You could buy a bay charger at the price I just named. But he merely tosses me a small sack of gold eagles, and says, "Make me believe it."

Soon, we strip him naked and strap him into the Maiden. He cannot even move his head. I say to him, "We must have a safeword for when it gets too rough. A code word we both agree will make me stop the show."

He looks at me with those terrible lime-green eyes, then says, "Darkish."

WYATT THRAILKILL

We KICKED IN a hornet's nest in Nashville. Them Yankees were caught by surprise, but they regrouped and druv us out the city the next day. We got some Nashville widows in our mess now, but we lost a whole heap of widows in the skirmishing on the old fairgrounds and throughout downtown. They fought well, but died all the same. I shirled into the fight and nigh lost my life a few spells. But I didn't come through this War to the other side just to die in Nashville. When I die, I die in Texas or not at all.

Cat won't call it a retreat. Maybe he's right, since we retreat north. But morale is low. We eke our way across the seven-hundred-foot-long wire suspension bridge that rises one hundred and ten feet over the Cumberland. Cat still rides that blasted Goliath that we have to somehow feed. He rides at the head of a column of warrior widows, orphans, circus freaks and now more than a heap of starving freed niggers who can't take the Freedom. I reckon I couldn't neither in 1865.

We cross the Cumberland uneasy. We don't know when the Yankee garrison will light out of the city proper to give battle again. All I know is that this side of the river is safe and that side of the river is not. That's all I know.

We strike camp in a meadow on the Bowling Green Road. Cat calls a council of war. The first in a long time. The first he calls with the women. He looks haggard and beat up, though it's hard to tell with the clown makeup he still wears. He has a map spread out on the massive back of Big Ugly, who remains hunched over like a table.

"We'll divide our regiment in two," he says, pointing at the map. "Worth, you and the Thrailkills lead your battalion: here and here till you reach Bowling Green. Captains O'Quinn and the Morton sisters will ride with you. The rest will ride with me. We'll meet in Bowling Green in three days. Any questions?"

"Who gits Big Ben?" Worth asks.

Cat waves his hand, as if to say, "Take it."

Then my brother, Gibby, says, "What about the gold?"

We grow stone silent. No one has talked about that there gold in the coffins since we took up with the widows a month ago. We all have watched it slowly turn into Cat Harvey's war chest. There must be $400,000 in those coffins.

"We already paid the widows last week," Cat says.

"I'm not talking about them bitches," Gib says. Some of the widow captains take offense. Brianna looks as though she'd liked to draw on my twin.

Cat smiles. He looks like a menacing clown with murder in his eyes. He says, "So it's mutiny then."

I step in. I know cause I don't talk often that Cat will listen to me and Gib will shut up. I tell Cat, "That gold is ours, not just yours. Ain't no mutiny in it."

"Tch," Cat says. "I care not a whit for gold. Take it. I'll meet y'all in Bowling Green."

Later that night, Gib and me are alone in our dog tent. And he says to me, "Wy, now's our chance."

"What chance?" I ask. He thinks just cause we's born twins that we can read each other's minds.

"You know," he says. "The gold."

I rise from my bedroll. "What do you mean *the gold*?"

"You know," Gib says. "Now's our chance."

He aims for us to steal it. I have never stolen anything in my life. Till now I hadn't even considered it.

Gib adds, raising his only arm, "Worth will come with us, too, I bet."

"You bet?" I say. "How do you aim we git past the widows?"

"They're not so tough."

"What happens when they find the gold missing? Where will we go?"

My twin brother points to the world outside our tent and says, "Anywhere we want."

SALOME

Miss Eliza won't eat. She looking mighty poorly. I tells her she gots to eat, but she won't listen to me; even though we been together since we's toddlers. Even though we's like sisters together. But something happened to Missy, and for the first time she don't confide in me.

We cross into Kentucky, I'm told, and half the widows ride under Mr. Worth, but we ride under Col. Cat. We cross into Kentucky, and that's when I hear the talk amongst the other maids. They never been this far north before. Then again, neither has me. I hear the talk for the first time, and for the first time I hear the word: "Freedom."

Once, when I was still a girl, I axed Miss Eliza if she would give me Freedom. Missy didn't slap my face. She didn't tell on me. She just said, "Salome, you already live under the protection of my liberty." I thought that was that. But now I hear the word cross the maid's lips in whispers. Some of the trashy freed niggas already make promises to them behind the colonel's back. If he learned what they's saying, Col. Cat would hang them from a sour apple tree. I wants to tell my Missy. I wants to tell her. But that word "Freedom" keeps me awake at nights and won't let me go.

Is the first secret I ever keep from Miss Eliza. Even though we's like sisters.

WORTH SOMERSETT

A FIRST LIEUTENANT GETS a hundred dollars in good hard money.
A second lieutenant gets ninety.
Third lieutenants get fifty.
First sergeants get twenty.
A second sergeant gets just nineteen dollars.
A third sergeant gets a dollar less.
A fourth sergeant, take away another dollar.
First corporals get blacksmith wages.
Second, third and fourth corporals get paid even less.

If you are a private in our command, then you don't even get a gold eagle for your trouble. We pay out in pesos.

There must be $500,000 in good hard money stacked in them coffins. Might could be. We never counted them. Gib Thrailkill says we can take it, that Cat Harvey is mad, and the gold is rightfully ours. We got but one chance and this is it. We are in Franklin, and Cat is in Scottsville. I listen to him, hard. It's like the serpent in the Garden. I listen to Gib like Jesus listened to the Devil when he offered him the whole, wide world.

A major makes more than two captains. But he still gets paid in pesos. What would the heft of a pawful of double eagles feel like in my hand? The heft might could tell me how much good hard money is in them coffins.

BRIANNA O'QUINN

Dɪᴅ ʜᴇ ᴛʜɪɴᴋ he could just take it? Did he think he could just reach out with that one arm of his and take our war chest? When every dog in the streets knows that our widows are made of stronger stuff, and that Banshee O'Quinn wouldn'a post a guard of inferior Shelias and Shannons. But the right smart bastard tried anyway. Gibby Thrailkill tried to steal our war chest with that one arm of his.

I hate all men ever since Cat Harvey did what he did to me on that bleeding night I choose not to remember. Maybe that's why I declared our widows a democracy when we captured the right smart bastard in Auburn. Did he think he could take it? Did he think when he held my Dubliner widows at gunpoint that they would quietly let him take them prisoner? The heathen. Oh, my two widows played along, Erin and Siobhan. They let him get in the back of the wagon and proceeded to light out east. Did the right smart bastard not think our pickets would suspect something when he said they rode out to forage? Or that Erin and Siobhan would not signal that something rotten was afoot as they passed? The heathen, and, ay!, with one arm!

They had not yet reached Auburn when my scouts captured them. Our widows formed a democracy on the spot.

"What do we do with thieves and deserters?" I asked them. And it was unanimous. Gibby Thrailkill would hang.

I didn'a ask for permission. I didn'a wait for Maj. Somersett or Capt. Thrailkill, the heathen's twin, to ride up to us. I put a rope around the

Thrailkill's neck, while my widows held him down, and hung him on the nearest hickory tree. T'was justice.

When Maj. Somersett and Capt. Thrailkill finally arrive on their galloping horses with a contingent of the Morton sisters' widows in tow, I stand my ground.

Wyatt Thrailkill dismounts before his horse comes to a full stop when he spots his one-armed twin swinging from that hickory tree. I wait for him to draw on me, for I will gun him down, too. But instead, he collapses on the ground. Disconsolate.

Then Worth Somersett shouts, "Brianna O'Quinn! On whose authority did you act?!"

"On the widows' authority," I say. I raise up my black dress and show him my sex. "And this is my badge!"

I could castrate the lot of them. Maj. Somersett doesn'a draw on me. He averts his eyes in the presence of my naked sex. He knows the widows in tow would gun him down, too. And Wyatt remains on the ground, half in the attitude of prayer, gazing upon the corpse of his brother twin.

But Worth Somersett says, "Wait till I tell Cat."

"Good," I declare. "Tell him, then. Tell him the widows have formed a democracy and willn'a be taking orders. Not without the vote."

POLK INGRAHAM

"SOMETHING HAS HAPPENED to one of your friends," Darkish says to me in the middle of the night. "Something bad." She roused me out of my tent just to tell me. Some think she's a witch. Others say she's blessed. I think she's the most mysterious gal I ever seen. I got a pug-nose and hers is a little upturned, too. She's so tiny, I feel like she might could fit in my two hands.

"Who?" I finally ask her. "What have you heard?"

"The rocks cried out, but I'm afraid to tell Col. Cat. He gets so angry."

"But you can tell me," I say. "And I can tell my cousin."

"One of the twins, the rocks didn't say his name. But I know it's one of the twins cause the rocks told me it was a one-armed man."

"Gibby?" I say. "Gibby Thrailkill?"

"They say he's dead over yonder," she says, solemn, mysterious.

I was raised to believe that you stayed away from witchcraft. If we's back in Texas, they'd call Darkish Llewellyn a *bruja*. But I say, "It was just a dream. It must be."

Darkish shakes her head. Her hair looks by turns black and blond in the moonlight.

"Go back to sleep, corporal," I tell her. "Leave me alone with your dreams."

She leaves me without another loving word. I return to my tent, but I cannot sleep. I'm amazed by her. I cannot sleep. Big Ugly snores piglet grunts in the tent. But that's not why I remain awake. I cain't git the tintype of Darkish's black and blond hair in the moonlight out of my mind. I feel the discomfort in my jean pants again. I stroke myself for aspell and then decide to chance it. I take out my flag of truce and commence stroking it, gentle at first, then real fast while Big Ugly snores away.

O Darkish, O Darkish! What color is your hair down there in the moonlight? What does it feel like to taste you down there? What does it feel like to go up under you down there?

JOSHUA CHAPMAN

THE REPORTS FROM Nashville were sketchy at best. Clowns, elephants, wild widows. Bowling Green hasn't seen much that one would call excitement since the Rebels evacuated the city at the start of the War. We took it for a joke. Something the boys in Nashville were playing on us to see if we'd take the bait. But when my captain said, "Better put a squadron on Vinegar Hill," I sensed a bit of trepidation in his voice. It made me wonder.

Vinegar Hill is haunted, or so the locals say. It rises two hundred or so feet above the Barren River, which affords a lovely view of the surrounding countryside. You would think that my men would enjoy the assignment. After all, there are plenty of cedars and limestone outcroppings to break up the monotony of other scenes. But they think Vinegar Hill is haunted. And here I thought Southerners were superstitious. Any snap of a branch or rustle in the underbrush and this would rouse one of my men. (I don't believe in ghosts. We don't have them in Indianapolis.) So many of my squad have "cried wolf" that I ordered them to cease with this ghost and goblin nonsense and get some sleep.

Now I'm awake. I hear noises of all sorts behind us, around us. I would sound a general alarm, except what sort of man would I be waking up the entire city because I thought I heard a ghost? So I wait. I want to wake up my squad, but then I think of the shame. So I wait. I hear something lumbering between the cedars, something ponderous with each step it takes. I want to whisper, "Do you hear that?" but I'm too ashamed of myself. Joshua Chapman. Get a hold of yourself. It's nothing but the wind.

Only there isn't any wind.

METTA DAHLGREN

Somehow I knew he would one day violate me. Somehow I always knew. All my widows are in love with the colonel, it seems. Cat Harvey is our champion. Yet he is no gentleman. He is a Confederate ghost, the inhuman avatar of 1865, sent to punish those who deigned to live with his "afflictions."

Bowling Green was our regiment's salient. I had taken it upon myself to record our deeds in poetry. (I am a captain, but I'm still a lady well-versed in the accomplishments.) It was a hit-and-run tactic. We had descended Vinegar Hill in a body at break of day, completely surprising the Yankee garrison and knocking them entirely off their guard. We were not there to liberate Bowling Green. "This city aggrieves me," Col. Cat said. "It's where my brother catched his pneumonia." For a moment, we thought the colonel might order the city burned down, and we widows would have obliged him. But instead, we recruited more Kentucky widows and pressed Kentucky horses. We loaded up our wagons with Yankee supplies.

Col. Cat would normally oversee it all, but he was in a state. He was running low on *Vin Mariani*, his "medicine." He needed more wine. We raided a wine cellar, but it would not do. Cat Harvey needed "coca," which gives him vitality. Finally, he found a druggist who sold him his precious *Vin Mariani* by the crateload. He practically gave it away to the boy colonel wearing a widow's dress, garish clown makeup and Colt revolvers.

It was on this matter that I decided to speak with Col. Cat. I am no Temperance woman. I know a man must take a drink, especially a Southern man. But I thought our colonel set a bad example for our ladies, some of whom dipped snuff with sticks. Disgusting. I sought him out to tell him that I thought he should be more mindful when he takes his medicine. Drink in front of officers, yes. But perhaps not in front of the rest of the ladies. I sought him out in the Daniel Boone Hotel. I sought him out, yet I felt in his presence summoned.

He was drinking his medicine. It never makes him drunk. It always leaves him dangerously alert.

"Colonel," I said. "I must speak with you."

"Oh Metta," he said. "What now?"

"I must come out and say it," I said. "Without hesitation. It is your drinking, sir. We all wish you would stop."

"You speak for the widows?" he said. He eyed me in a most ferocious way. He took another swig of his medicine.

"I feel I do. I feel it is bad for morale to watch you hurt yourself with spirits."

"You feel?" he said. "You *feel?* Captains don't feel, Metta; they *think.*"

I was confused. So I said, "Then I think—"

"That I am a drunk."

"No, sir," I said. But then I added, "I think you are in pain."

He took another swig of his medicine before pronouncing, "In pain? What all do you know about my pain? You flounce in here wearing a turban like some aristocrat's belle and axpect me to call you captain and tell you my pain?! I'm a man of honor—I don't feel nothing no more! But you certainly will!"

And that's when it happened. I'm still too much a lady to say what happened next, or perhaps I simply choose not to remember. Cat Harvey violated me, is all. The supreme insult of the War. And now I find myself having to *pull yourself together, Metta.* Just like I did when Sherman's bummers burned my home to ashes. I find myself making excuses for the colonel. "He was drunk," I say to myself. "Men can't help themselves when they're drunk." Or I say to myself, "You must have provoked him. After all, you wore your Moab and are known to flirt. You must have flirted with him." But this cannot be true.

I have never felt so ruined.

ETHAN BRIARSTONE

I HAVE BEEN HELD captive now not two weeks, yet I already see my chances of survival dwindling. Cat Harvey has no interest in ransoming me. I am his guest. I am under his hospitality for the duration. I plot my escape daily, hourly even; yet I know it is futile. Cat Harvey's regiment of widows, who have begun calling themselves a brigade, are too numerous. What few men are in camp, like myself, stand out. So I try to find new ways to make myself useful to this deranged soul. I make him believe I am going to file a report with the *Herald* once he sets me free. I make him believe that I am there to interview him, as if I truly am his guest.

I tramp with the boy colonel to the mouth of Mammoth Cave. I fear I am in the most danger whenever we are alone, but I know that as long as I make myself useful to him Cat Harvey will keep me alive. At least I pray this is so.

It is eerily cool at the mouth of this cave, as my captor eyes me with an appraising look.

"Wordsworth," he says. "Ask your questions."

"Why did you leave Bowling Green after liberating it from its garrison?" I ask.

"Cause I airn't here to hold territory," he replies. "We's all nomads now. Our horses and mules is our country."

I write this down, then ask, "What is your military objective?"

"My plan?" he says. "My plan is to burn Tecumseh Sherman's home after my widows have rained hellfire on Northrop's Scouts."

"Why not burn Sherman's home first?" I ask.

Cat Harvey reflects on this question a moment, then says, "You sound like one of my widows, Ethan Briarstone." This is the first time he has ever said my name. "No one understands me, it seems. Mutiny in the air. I'll tell you what: I'll not burn Sherman's home till I render the Scouts dead. We savor him for last."

"Yes, but why?"

"Cause when news reaches Tecumseh Sherman that his precious Scouts's massacred and their homes is burnt to cinders, he'll cast about like a trapped bear. I *want* him to cast about. I *want* him to know what it means to know Hell is coming. Hell is not eternal punishment. It is the long wait for inevitable retribution."

I write this down, too. I am about to ask him something else, but then he proceeds to interview me. He says, "I read your journal. Ever word. Found it in your tricks."

I don't know why I am surprised or offended, but before my mouth gets the best of me, I clamp tight my jaws.

"Yes," Cat Harvey says. "I read your journal so I might could better play host to you. It says you're Unitarian. I was raised Presbyterian, myself."

"Then you must know that I am not here in the South as a soldier or a war profiteer. I'm a journalist."

"A *Unitarian* journalist," he corrects.

I am used to such prejudices against my faith, so I simply nod.

"Y'all don't believe in the trinity," he declares. "Y'all don't believe that Jesus Christ were the son of God. Y'all don't believe in salvation. What do y'all believe in then?"

"Redemption," I say. And this one word could have knocked Cat Harvey back on his haunches.

He turns his head counterclockwise to the side, and asks, "What did you say?"

"Redemption," I repeat. "That no man is beyond redemption."

He considers me a moment, then says, "I've heard that word before. You're my second prisoner what tell that to me."

"Then you must have considered it," I say, though I sense the danger in pressing him.

Cat Harvey closes his eyes and places his left hand gently on his cheek. He looks as stony as the cave itself. When he finally opens his eyes, he tells me, "Yes, I've considered it. I would very much like to be redeemed. It would be monstrous nice to think so. But if you knew half the things I done in this War...*I'm* beyond redemption. Write that down."

I refuse. There are some principles more important than the first one: to live. I refuse to write down that Cat Harvey is beyond redemption.

"No?" he says. "You defy me?" He laughs like the clown he appears to be.

"No man is beyond redemption," I say. "Not even you."

"Bullshit," he says. "It's Unitarian bullshit. Comes from Yankee Devil worship, I reckon."

"You're agitated," I say. "Why. What makes you so agitated? Because you were one of Shannon's Scouts? What did you do in the War? What is it you did that makes you believe now that you are beyond redemption?"

Cat Harvey draws his gun on me for an answer. "I am not redeemed," he says. His voice is cold. "My afflictions are too great. I seen Christ burn up on his cross in a Georgia cornfield with a murder of crows hovering over him. I committed a heap of wrongthings, *things you do not do*; and now I must suffer the consequences. I am damned, you hear me? *Damned.*"

I shake my head "no." If he shoots me on the spot, then so be it. I will not tolerate this faulty line of reasoning.

Cat Harvey does not fire his Colt revolver. Instead, he says, "You really would let me shoot you. You really believe your own bullshit."

"I don't believe in much," I declare. "But what I do believe in I shall die knowing it is true."

Cat Harvey holsters his weapon. He looks into the cave for one long moment, then says, "Well, Wordsworth. Then I must show you."

DARKISH LLEWELLYN

A CAVE IS A hollowed out rock. It contains all the secrets of the rock, but cain't help but tell them. After all, it's still a cave. They think Mammoth Cave is old and will keep them safe. But this rock's heart is still young inside. It speaks to me with a child's voice.

I know he has followed me ever since I slunk out of camp. The moon is not so bright tonight. At first, I fear it is Cat, but the cave tells me it's his cousin, Polk. It tells me he's in love with me, the shaver. It tells me Polk is a good boy. He might could protect me from Cat. So I let him follow me all the way to the mouth of the cave. I light my candle and proceed to walk inside, when

"Psst!" I hear from twenty paces away. "Darkish," he says. "Don't be scairt. It's me, Capt. Ingraham."

"I know it's you, Polk," I say. "You may come to me."

He approaches me like a dog that is not sure he's about to get a treat. I proceed into the cave. It tells me this is a good man. That his heart is pure. That he would defend me from a lion, much less a Cat.

"What are you doing, girl?" he says. The cave echoes his words. "It's too dark in here. It ain't safe." The cave tells me Polk is scared I might be scared. Tells me he's a good man. That his heart is true.

I tell him, "The rock cried out and won't let me sleep. It said it has something to show me in its belly."

"What if there's a bear in here, Darkish?" he says. But he ain't scared. He thinks I should be cause I'm a girl. I wonder if I might could love this boy.

"The rock cried out," I simply say. He follows my every step. Sometimes the cave opens wide, like I imagine a plantation house's foyer. Other times the cave closes on us, like my measly shack back in Ringgold.

"What're you looking for?" Polk asks. He is afraid to come too close to me. The cave tells me he's a good man. That if I marry him, he'd give me a heap of sweet young'uns. That his heart is pure and true.

I tell him, "The rock cried out. It wants to show me something inside its belly. That's all I know."

The candle does not burn bright, but we can still see. We can see the cave droppings from its roof and the cave risings from its floor. The rock tells me Polk Ingraham is a sweet, sweet boy. That I keep him up at night with his wonderings about me. That he'd make a fine husband, if I marry him. That he would be a tenderness to me.

Then we come upon what looks like a wall. At first, I think it is snakes crawling down it. But then I say, "It's just writing. Look."

And Polk says, "I see."

We inspect the wall. Names and dates. Names and dates in different hands.

"How did they write in the rock?" I ask. The cave does not answer me. It tells me instead that Polk Ingraham has a strong, pure heart. That he will protect me when Cat Harvey attacks.

Polk takes the candle out of my hand and proceeds to shine an empty space on the wall. We both watch the wall get sooty. Then Polk writes: "*Polk & Darkish, 1865.*"

I step over to him and kiss him. He like to drop the candle. His pure, true heart is pounding in his chest against my right breast. I open my eyes when we finish our kiss and spot another name on the wall: *Henry Clay Somersett, 1843.* I scream. The cave does not have to tell me, I know; it merely echoes my scream.

"What is it, Darkish?" Polk cries. He holds me. But I point to the name on the wall. Polk is astonished. He lets go of me to inspect the name for certain.

"That's the name," I say. "The name of the ha'nt that haunts your cousin."

But Polk turns round and says, "It cain't be. It just cain't be. That there is the name of my sister's husband."

HANDSOME

THE BELL, ROLL CALL, then off to the canteen for the thin gruel we call breakfast. Oakland plantation feeds us nigs just enough to keep us working, just enough to keep us alive. I thought I was a shade flitting through the nightworld. Now I know that I'm a nig hoping to survive twilight.

That infernal bell again. It tells us it's time. Our work detail assembles in a two-rowed line facing the gate. None of us want the lash. Our Negro guards post themselves in front of and behind our line. One shouts, "All right, nigs! March!"

We mark time until our guards move forward, then we march to the gate which opens for us. Above the gate the sign reads: *THE HAND OF THE DILIGENT SHALL BEAR RULE: BUT THE SLOTHFUL SHALL BE UNDER TRIBUTE.* We do not know which of the fields we shall work: tobacco, hemp, rice, sugar or cotton. The punishment is random, yet it all amounts to the same. We are nigs, the numbers on our backs. But I am not a number! I am Henry Clay Somersett! I must remind myself my name, lest I forget it here.

The day-dawn is particularly bright for those of us who have been on Oakland plantation for as long as a second life. One almost wants to stop and admire it. But to fall out of line means certain death. And none of us wish to return to the nightworld.

Yet the march is monotonous, tedious even. The only thoughts that occupy my mind are those of my dreams. Nightmares, they seem. But dreams compared to the twilight to which I awaken. Last night I dreamt I was Cat

Harvey again, as always, but this time I also dreamt of Mammoth Cave. My Kentucky home.

"*05031971!*" a guard shouts. He gives me the lash and I howl in agony. "Eyes forward!"

"Yes, master!" I tell him. "Thank you, master!"

I have to be more careful with my daydreaming. I could accidentally step out of line, and then what? I resolve to wait until we reach our worksite. We pass through rows and rows of fields where other work details slave under the lash. Yet just when we believe we have reached ours, we are turned west where we eventually arrive at our site. There is plenty of timber and tools.

"All right, nigs!" another guard shouts. "Grab a tool and get to work!"

They don't have to tell me what we are building. We are building another prison.

GEORGE SOMERSETT

I₈ ᴛʜᴇ Nᴀᴍᴇ of God, Amen, I, George Washington Somersett, of the County of Hart, and Commonwealth of Kentucky, being at this time in my proper senses, make but also calling to mind the Mortality of my Body being also in a low Condition of Health, do ordain this my last will and Testament In manner and form follows Viz—

First, I Commend my Soul into the Hands of the Almighty God who gave it to me, and my Body to the earth from whence it was Taken—

Second, I will that my Just debts and funereal expenses be paid and Satisfied.

Item   I give and bequeath unto my beloved wife Sarah Somersett my negro man Flynn valued at $600 to her and unto her heirs and assigns. I also give and bequeath unto my wife all my stock of horses, cattle and hogs and my house Somersett Hall with all my house furniture and plantation tools of every kind and all my provisions.

I lend unto my beloved wife Sarah Somersett during her natural life my negro woman called Peg valued at $300.

Item   I give and bequeath unto my eldest son Henry Clay Somersett absolutely nothing should he still be alive. I hereby command my heirs to shun him for his service in that traitorous Confederacy.

Item   I give and bequeath unto my son Zachary Taylor Somersett my negro girl called Betsey valued at $200 to him and to his heirs and assigns.

Item   I give and bequeath unto my son John Tyler Somersett one hundred acres of land lying near the head of Cane Swamp to him and his heirs and assigns forever. I give and bequeath unto my said son my mulatto boy called Joseph valued at $250 before lent unto my wife, to be delivered to him at the death of my wife and to his heirs and assigns.

Item   I give and bequeath unto my youngest son John Wesley Somersett absolutely nothing. I hereby command my heirs to shun Worth for his service in that traitorous Confederacy. Moreover, I hereby Renounce his right to bear the honorable name Somersett, for riding with a band of widow partisans under the villain known as Galveston.

And   I hereby make and ordain my two worthy friends Brutus Williams and Jerome Bell executors of this my last will and testament. In witness whereof I the said George Washington Somersett have to this my last will and testament set my hand and seal the day and year June 30, 1865.

FAYETTE ABERNATHY

I ALLOW THEM TO camp on my plantation for one night only because my nephew Worth rides with them. George, my brother-in-law, has disowned him entirely. It was the same way he did with Clay during the War. Worth rode up to George's tobacco farm, his home, and waited by the gateposts for one of his darkies to come, I'm told. They exchanged messages. In the end, Worth was not even allowed to see his own mother, my sister, who I know has not seen her boy for nigh on a year. George has always had a hard heart, especially when it comes to politics. When they say the War was brother against brother, they must have meant Kentucky.

I am not so old as to say that I have seen it all, but I've seen my share. Yet behold: Cat Harvey. He goes by the sobriquet: Galveston, the Rodeo Clown. He parades himself in a black widow's dress and clown makeup like one of his circus freaks. I lost all my sons in the War, all five of them. They rode with John Hunt Morgan. Worth saw two of them die. But now I see that they were better off dead because who keeps up the Cause? There is not a word invented yet to describe Cat Harvey and his "Widows' Brigade."

I tolerate them. I tolerate talking to a grown boy in a dress and armed women. Why do I tolerate them? Because they keep the flame alive. My sons didn't die in vain, so long as someone, anyone, even Cat Harvey, rides north.

They must surely die. But that is how glory is made.

What is a Southern man to do but throw a barbeque? I am famous in all of Hart County for my mutton barbeque and Derby pie. I apologize to Cat Harvey (I cannot bring myself to call the boy "colonel") for not having enough beeves to make Texas brisket. We talk of the barbeque he has seen in his travels throughout the South: Mississippi, Alabama, Tennessee, Georgia, the Carolinas. Makes my mouth water, though I prefer my Kentucky style.

Then I take the boy aside. I say, "Come, let me show you my horse pasture." Once there, I say to the boy, "You know how fond I am of my nephew."

"Yes sir," he says. "Worth is a fine major."

"Son," I say, "what are you doing arming young widows and gallivanting around in widow's weeds yourself?"

He does not burn with shame. How can a man have honor without a sense of shame? Instead, he replies, "Yes. I am Galveston now. I am an island unto myself which no man can conquer. I wear these widow's weeds cause the world has done turnt upside down and tipped over. But do not mistake me for a sissy. Like my widows, I carry a brace of pistols on my person. And I have nigh exhausted my ammunition."

I believe the boy must be crazy insane. I fear for Worth. He is no widow. He is just a boy of eighteen, my nephew.

"How old are you, Cat?" I ask.

"Nineteen, sir," he replies. "I were fifteen when I joint the Rangers. Eighteen when I joint Shannon's Scouts with Henry Clay."

"You rode with Clay?" I ask. "Then surely you know what happened to him?"

He grows solemn and quiet. He stares at the horses in my pasture. Then he says, "There is a gal in our outfit what talks to rocks. And the rocks talk back. She held a long Texas chat with Mammoth Cave, as you can imagine. Some of my widows think she's a witch. Mebbe I do, too. Darkish Llewellyn is her name, and Darkish tells me Clay Somersett is a ghost what haunts me now. I'm demonized, she says. Why, she doesn't know. But I do."

"I don't want to hear any more of this," I say. I nigh send him off of my property.

But he goes on to say, "We in the Scouts are now damned cause what we performed during the War. If Clay Somersett's an angel now, he's a angel of retribution. Like as not, he's in Hell. Which is where I'm bound. I cain't axcape it."

I have heard enough. I march myself away from the pasture. I want to run. Run into the house, take the musket off my mantel and shoot Cat Harvey like the rabid dog I believe he is. T'would be mercy. But I am overcome with grief. My nephew, Henry Clay, damned. Is it possible? I am a man of honor. I don't believe in Heaven and Hell. I believe in one's name and own blood. But what has become of the name, Henry Clay Somersett? My own blood. Sister must never know what became of her son. That, had he lived, Clay Somersett would like as not wear clown makeup and a dress alongside Cat Harvey. *Deranged.* What could they have possibly done, those Scouts? No, it is unthinkable! I refuse to think on it anymore.

I march to the head of my table, sit down, and proceed to feast on barbequed mutton until I'm good and stuffed. Then thoughts of my nephew reappear. So I get a second helping and eat until I can forget.

VELLA MORTON

Brianna O'Quinn has called a secret meeting of the widow captains in Mr. Abernathy's smokehouse. She has been a pariah to the colonel ever since she hung Gibby Thrailkill, despite saving Cat Harvey's war chest. He strung her up by her thumbs, "put her on roots," and let her hang aspell herself. Like to haul off and hit him. I know he did something to Miss Bee, something she won't say. Like to haul off and hit him.

We are all present, all except for my sister. (Marietta flat refuses to do what I say ever since I helped them take her arm.) Brianna stares at Eliza, Elisha, Metta and me. This makes us anxious and oneasy. Then Brianna says, "Col. Cat is mad as a hatter."

No one disputes this. Yet we're afraid to nod in agreement.

"Three of my widows are in the family way because of him," she adds. "The colonel raped them, just like he *raped* my mouth."

All eyes grow wide with recognition. It dawns on me that that is what he must of done to poor Miss Bee! I could kill him. I could haul off and kill him!

"You must be mistaken," Metta says, her voice quavering. "The colonel would never do such a thing."

Brianna looks deep into Metta's eyes and then says, "Didn'a he now? Do you call me a liar, then?"

Metta's feathers are in a ruffle. She says, "It never happened. The colonel would never…" but she cannot finish. All of us realize that he did do such a thing, and to *her*.

"Tell us, Metta," Brianna says. "Tell us what the monster colonel did."

One of us reaches out to touch Metta's shoulder, but she backs away. There's tears in her eyes, but she refuses to squall out.

Then Elisha Tooke tells Metta, "I know what Cat did cause he did it to me."

But Eliza Reed says, shaking her head, "We shouldn't be here, meeting like this! What if he finds us? What if we get caught?"

"What more can he do to us," Brianna replies, "that the beast hasn'a already done?"

"It was my fault," Eliza says. "Men can't help themselves once you provoke them. It was entirely my fault."

Now Metta speaks. "He is no gentleman," she says. "There is nothing gentle about Cat Harvey at all."

"Right," Brianna says. "Which is why we widows must form a democracy together. We must strike at Cat Harvey in unison."

"But what about Sherman?" I hear myself say. It's as if the entire smokehouse is a great big hall, the sound is so loud. We remain quiet for one long minute.

"What about the heathen Sherman?" Brianna says. "Are we not capable of marching on Ohio ourselves? Do you not think a widow can strike a match and burn the heathen's house just as surely as a man? Speak, Vella!"

"Quiet," Eliza says. "He might hear us."

"Let him hear," Metta declares. "Our voices must be heard."

"Right," Brianna says. "Then we are resolved. The colonel must go. Then we march together on Ohio and burn the heathen's house to ashes."

But then Elisha Tooke protests. "What about the Tennessee widows? What about the Kentucky ones? What makes us think they're loyal to us Georgians?"

"They'll fall in line, to be sure," Brianna says.

Elisha asks more of her questions, questions we don't have answers for yet. She grows monstrous nervous. I can smell her fear through the constant scent of mutton. Then Elisha asks, "How will we git close enough to kill him?"

But it is as if all of us have the same answer on our tongue: *Jincy*.

"That Mountain girl goes into the colonel's tent at night," Metta says. "I know what they do. I know."

"Yes," Brianna says. "But would she help us?"

None of us have an answer. We's only resolved to kill Col. Cat, the man that raped every widow in the smokehouse but me.

JOHN HENRY HOLIDAY

I AM DOC HOLIDAY. The colonel has made it so. My voice has changed since we crossed the Green River. It's so squeaky now that I dare not speak, not even to Uncle Calsas. He asks me questions, and I mumble back my answers, but I dare not speak up. I'm too ashamed.

Ever since I pulled the wrong tooth from out the colonel's mouth, I've had the same dream at night. I'm holding the pair of pliers, and every widow in camp, it seems, is looking at me and then my teeth commence falling one by one out my mouth. I drop the pliers and try to speak, but my squeaky voice is so bad that the widows laugh at me. They all laugh at me! Then I wake up, always checking to see if my teeth are still there in my mouth.

I must be an orphan now, like so many of the real ones that follow us on the march. I am a wayfarer on the road to perdition. Yet do I follow.

We make camp along the river south of Bardstown. The widows are in a bad way. English Measles. Half the camp is down sick, it seems. Liked to happen overnight. Four of the widows, two orphans and a circus juggler already died from them. Now the widows that ain't sick are nurses to the ones that are. Constant worry is on everyone's face but Uncle Calsas's. He goes on shoeing horses or breaking the ones we press. I want to ask him why he's not scared, but I dare not speak up. I'm too ashamed.

I am Doc Holiday now, four hundred miles from all I have ever known.

BEE BREWSTER

I'M SICK WITH English Measles. I am weak and covered in spots. Vella watches over me, tenderly. Every time I have a coughing fit, she cries.

"Why do you cry, Vella?" I finally say.

"Miss Bee," she replies. "If I told you the reason, then you wouldn't be my friend no more."

I assure her that that would never happen, could never happen, but Vella continues to cry as she watches over me. I must know the reason by now. Vella has fallen in love with me, but she cannot say it with words. Words would make it real. It is the same reason that keeps me from telling her why I am afraid of Cat Harvey. I have kept my hair shorn like a boy's to make me less attractive to the world of men. No one will attack you if you look like a boy, I told myself. But now it seems that Vella has fallen in love with me, though she cannot bring herself to say it aloud. Words become cudgels when what we want are instruments and tools.

"Please don't die on me, Miss Bee," Vella says. "I just couldn't bear it."

"You, Vella?" I say. "But you're so very strong. You and Marietta are two of the toughest widows in our brigade."

"No, I am not. I act tough cause I'm a captain, but I'm not so tough. Not on the inside."

I cough again. I cannot make myself stop.

"Miss Bee," Vella says with tears blearing her eyes. "Do you think I might could kiss you?"

"I'm sick with measles, Vella," I say. "It would be unwise."

"I won't git sick," she says. "I never git sick. I'm too hardy."

I want to tell her "no," but I'm so very weak. And Vella has been so good to me as my captain, so very good to me. I believe I love her, though not in the way I know she is with me. Yet ever since Cat Harvey… ever since that night… if only I could make my beauty invisible to the world.

But Vella sees my beauty, despite my shorn hair; and she has not attacked me, though she so desires me. I'm confused and feverish, yet if Vella were to lean down and kiss me I would push her away. I would muster the strength to push her away. But she doesn't. She waits for me to answer, but does not move. If I were to speak, I'd tell her "No." I would send her away. But who else in the world cares for me, Little Bee Brewster? No one came to my rescue the night in the cupola when Cat Harvey struck.

I raise my torso. I surprise Vella. I take her hand and then kiss her. I surprise myself. It is a brief kiss and does not feel like the way it does with boys. But it is still a kiss, a compact.

"When you git better, like I know you will," Vella tells me, "I'm gonna kill Cat Harvey. I'm gonna kill him and then it won't matter what happens next."

SMIT HARVEY

GOLIATH, THE ELEPHANT, has died. Let us drink to that! Let us drink to this accursed Life that brought into the world a baby elephant somewhere in the wilds of darkest Africa and then snatched him up—took him—sailed him across the sea, like so many Negroes, and then worked him into performing all sorts of unnatural tasks for men, like my little brother, till he died where Terry's Texas Rangers once fought the Battle of Bardstown in the Commonwealth of Kentucky. The widows are dying of English Measles, and I am dying of thirst. So let us drink to Death!

He was not an overly clean elephant. He was not even the biggest in all of America. But Goliath was a sturdy pack animal—that he was! And his trumpet was a call to arms!

I am somewhat in liquor. I am in my cups. But I do not drink cocaine, like my little brother has taken to imbibing of late. I will not touch that *Vin Mariani*. It's *poison*, and I told Catullus so. His "medicine," he calls it. I call it poison. And if he didn't have two hulking Mountain widows guarding his supply, I would dynamite the whole lot of it.

We are so close to *Lou*ville that I can practically hear the roulette wheels spinning. I have not played a decent hand of faro in an age. I have lost large sums at faro, but I have also won plenty. Some in my family say I drink owing to the fact that I gamble; others, that I gamble because I drink. My vices are my affair. I am not so philosophical that I shall rationalize them away. But they are still *mine*.

We call ourselves a brigade, but in reality we are a Confederate brigade.

Perhaps it is what the cruel gods want. *Vanitas vanitatum, omnia vanitas!* The measles has decimated our numbers, and now our elephant is dead. Let us drink to Goliath, who surely did not die of the measles but rather of malnutrition. To Goliath! Who served the Confederacy well. Such a pachyderm would have gladly trampled on Gen. Sherman's front yard, if he'd have lived. But alas, the cruel gods took him. And my little brother had the audacity to take out his bowie knife and amputate Goliath's tusks.

There lay the poor beast. Poor, poor Goliath. No David struck you down, but the myriad Davids of starvation and malnutrition. You deserved a more honorable death. Yet now you are tuskless, just like me. We are brothers, you and I. When Bob Hill cut off my leg with his bone-saw at Bentonville, I lost my tusks. Poor Goliath. *Ad meliora vertamur.*

BRIANNA O'QUINN

T'IS A PLAGUE, it is. Yankees to the south of us. Yankees to the north of us. Yankees abound. And we are suffering the sickness that I know is God's plague. I was prepared to kill Cat Harvey myself, the Devil in a man's shape, when the measles rained down on us and covered my widows with so many spots a leopard wouldn'a be surprised. I was prepared to kill him myself for raping my mouth that night on Lookout Mountain. (I can still taste him.) But I have seen the sign. God is full of wrath because the widow captains have conspired against our colonel, the Chosen One. It breaks my Irish heart, but I have seen the sign and read it. We chose Cat Harvey, and all that comes with the beast.

But now I look a fool for my trepidations. I look weak in the eyes of my conspirators. We took an oath in that smokehouse, a blood oath at that. How can I call the whole thing off?

Elisha Tooke asks her questions. "How are we to stop it now?" she asks. "What are we to do?" she asks, afeared for herself. She isn'a a coward though. Elisha simply doesn'a want to get raped again.

"You think I don'a want to cut off his balls and feed them to the man?" I say. Metta Dahlgren and Eliza Reed, the ladies, flinch at hearing such talk. But we are widows, not ladies.

But it is Vella Morton who raises an objection. Imagine, Vella Morton, the last one to raise her hand in the smokehouse! She says, "Omen or not, I aim to kill Cat Harvey fore the moon gits full."

"Then we are all doomed," I declare. "You might as well kill yourself in the bargain."

"You Irish," she says. T'is all she has to say for I to hit her. I knock big, stocky Vella Morton on her big, stocky arse. All eyes gaze at me in wide wonder. I stand over her and show her my fist.

"Vella Morton!" I say. "Hear me now, you Sapphic bull! I will kill any widow that says a word against the Irish!"

Vella scrambles up to her feet. She's furious; but no, she doesn'a charge me. Instead, she leaves the circle of our conspiracy in a great huff.

"What say the rest of you?" I demand. But the rest of the widow captains have grown dumb.

Then it is Metta's turn to speak, the lady. She says, "You expect us to take this outbreak as a sign, Brianna, an omen. But what if it is God's way of testing our resolve?"

Yet before I can give reply, Elisha Tooke says, "Suppose'n there ain't no God. Suppose'n we have to decide for ourselves."

"Elisha Tooke!" Metta declares. "Bite your tongue!"

But Cat Harvey has released us all our tongues to freely wag. Elisha says, "If there was a God in the sky, why did He let Sherman burn our homes? Why did He leave us unprotected like that? Why did He afflict Col. Cat with the soldier's heart and let him ruin us, like He did?"

Metta rears back to slap Elisha, but I grab hold of her wrist. She still says, "What are you saying, Elisha? What are you trying to say?"

But now Eliza, not Elisha, speaks. "She's saying that we decide our fates, not our girlhood notions of God. Those were pleasant dreams, but 1865 changed all of that. We are awakened. Now we must decide for ourselves the fate of Cat Harvey."

"We know how Vella votes," Metta says. "And I vote with her. Cat Harvey must die. It's for the Cause. Remember the Cause!"

"Then I vote no," Elisha Tooke says. "Cat Harvey has led us this far. He will lead us to Sherman, sure enough. We just have to guard each other in the meantime."

"As vote I," say I. "God has put His curse on this conspiracy. We must resign ourselves to it and prepare ourselves for the day when we burn the heathen Sherman's home to its foundation."

We turn and look to Eliza Reed. We are a democracy of widows and her vote decides us. Eliza clutches her belly, then touches her temples. We wait impatiently for her to decide.

"It is not so simple for me," she finally says. "I loved the colonel once. Now I hate him just as much."

"Then it's settled," I say.

But Eliza says, "No. It's not so simple."

"Why, Eliza?" we all seem to ask.

She looks down at her belly, her eyes behold it, and then she says, "I am with child."

UNCLE CALSAS

Now he act like we friends. Mr. Cat been mighty crazy on this here campaign of his. He oughts to act like he a man. But he dress just like a rodeo clown, and a hush gonna fall over Jerusalem when he finish with the bull, Bill Sherman. Now he act like we friends. Like it won't him who stood and watch whilst he brother Sul took the hatchet to my fretting hand. Mr. Cat stood there and watch. I might be an old wall-eyed nigga, my time is nigh coming, but I ain't never gonna forget the look on Cat Harvey's face in my only time of need.

Now he act like we friends. He come sauntering up to me when I got work to do. He see that plain as day. But he takes the bench I use on the march and sets it down like a gangplank. Then he put he back to me and sets hisself down. He act like we friends, like we still friends. I know what I'm axpected to do. He axpects me to turn my back to his'n, to set myself on the gangplank bench, and talk to him man-to-man instead of man-to-nigga.

So I obleege him. Why, I don't rightly know. Mebbe I been doing it so long I cain't stop now. Mebbe I just want to hear Cat Harvey out. Learn what he aims to do with an old nigga like Uncle Calsas. So I set myself down on the bench, my back to his'n. If we was standing up, I'd say we was erbout to fought a duel.

He start. He always start. "You think I'm mad, don'cha?"

"I reckon not," I says.

"But you think I'm mad," he say. "You think I dress this way to look like a clown. But it's just my afflictions, Calsas. They taunt and haunt me."

"I gots work to do, Mr. Cat," I says. "What all do you want now with me?"

"I know you want to go back to Texas."

I try not to think on Texas. I try not to think of my sweet Serena. Cause when I do I commence to feeling poorly. Too much salt in my sweet bread.

Mr. Cat say, "You don't have to answer me, if you don't want. I know you miss Serena, specially since you cain't play your mandolin no more."

"All I play now is my blues," I says.

"You hate me," he say. "Go on, I can take it."

"What you whitefolks don't understand," I says. "What you never understand, is how little I *do* think of you."

I rise up from the gangplank bench. We finish. I always finish.

SPENCER HEWITT

" *WATER!*" I WHISPER hoarsely when I mean to shout. Nobody answers me. They all lay dead. You had survived the War, Spencer Hewitt, despite seeing your share of the fight. From Donelson to Bentonville. You rode under some of the worst generals, but still rode under the one true flag. You thought it an act of grace when you returned home to Louville a hero. All the Rebs in Kentucky were good and dead. John Hunt Morgan, nothing but the next Benedict Arnold. Now the South would finally join the Union. Death to the slavers. Free soil for free labor. Oh, Spencer, you saw your post in Louville as an auspicious sign, didn't you? Now you lay dying amongst a pile of your dead brothers-in-arms.

Our captain thought we were so smart. A raped widow had escaped Galveston's camp, somewhere in Bardstown, and she told the whole story. That there were armed widows riding north to burn Yankee homes and kill Gen. Sherman. That most were down sick with measles and other camp diseases. That this Galveston, the Rodeo Clown was a mere boy of nineteen. Our captain laughed, he actually laughed, when he heard this. The poor widow, however, didn't think it was funny.

"He raped me!" she said.

"Serves you right, Rebel," he said. Then he had our guards lock her up for safekeeping. I wanted to protest, I should have protested; but I thought he might do the same to me. I thought of my promotion to a commissioned officer. I would be alive now if I were to have spoken up on that poor widow's behalf. I would be alive now instead of bleeding out in this damned field.

We were so haughty. You looked to your promotion, Spencer Hewitt. Now it is assured, you thought. And all you have to do is just shoot your Enfield and scare away a few mad bitches. Our captain said to us, as we rode south, "These Rebel girls. They're worse than their men." We laughed. We actually laughed.

We had no idea how true his words were.

I wonder where the captain is now. Is he somewhere in the heap, or did he escape? If I could spot him under one of the heaps of horses and men, I'd shoot him myself; that is, if I could find my rifle. If I could just have some damn water!

"*Water!*" I whisper hoarsely without raising a shout.

"Here's one!" I hear a woman shout. I raise my head as best I can and see it is a widow. She has the measles, yet she is strong enough to stride toward me and level her shotgun.

"Water!" I whisper, though why I don't know.

"Water don't make you no difference now, Yankee," she says. She cocks her shotgun. "How do you want it? Quick or slow?"

"Water!" I whisper. "Please."

"Please and thank yous is over," she says. "I reckon you want it quick."

But before she opens fire, I look into her eyes and say, "I know why the widows run."

She ports her shotgun. "What did you say?" she demands.

"The widows," I say. "I know why they run from him."

"Jincy!" a widow's voice is heard in the distance. But this Jincy does not answer. I expect her to point her shotgun at me, but instead she strides forward and steps over me. "Jincy!" the other widow shouts.

"False alarm!" Jincy says. "I thought we had a live one."

Now I am to bleed out. If only I would have spoken up back in Louville. If only I had some water. Yet I am too weak to even shout "Jincy!" and beg for my death.

SALOME

Miss Eliza is in the family way. She get sick when she least expect it then turn beet red cause ladies don't get sick in public. The niggas on the march talk to each other in hushes and whispers. They's at least two hundred of us now. Soon we cross the Ohio. Soon we cross into Freedom. I is so confused. I don't know what to do. My Missy, she need me. And she say I already free but living under her liberty ain't the same as Freedom. Some of the niggas, the scared ones, whisper, "What I want with Freedom? Ain't Marse Lincoln already set us free?" but then another one will say, "Freedom in the North. Be a good nigga till then."

Miss Eliza say, when we's alone, "It was my fault. It was entirely my fault."

"What is, Missy?" I say.

"Oh, Salome," she say. "I wish I were home. I want to go home!"

But Sherman burn the only home we had.

I say, "I know your secret, Missy. It awright, I won't tell nobody."

"Oh, Salome," she say again. "What am I to do?" She throw her arms around my neck and cry. Back in Georgia, when we had a home, I would soothe Missy with a song my Mammy sing to me. But don't have no song in my heart for Miss Eliza no more. I emancipated from her, though we growed up like sisters. Freedom grow in my heart just as big and strong as that baby that's in Missy's belly. And I know who the father is, too.

"Bide your time," the niggas whisper. "We cross the Ohio soon. On Independence Day."

METTA DAHLGREN

Our darkies took action where we captains could not. Imagine our surprise, our shock indeed. Here I thought my maid, Flora—whom I gave a pair of gold bobs to and let sleep at the foot of my bed on a mattress, mind—here I thought Flora would stay loyal at my side. Freedom is a madness. Poor Flora must have been caught up in it. When the rest of the darkies revolted and attempted to bolt after we crossed the Ohio into Yankeedom, she must have been swept away in the madness of it all. "Someone needs to wash the Africa off that gal," Mother would say whenever I tried, as a child, to call Flora a lady. I now must concede that Mother was right.

Yet they nearly did what we widow captains hadn't the courage to do: kill Cat Harvey. Two buck negroes attacked him in his sleep with machetes. (Where they got these weapons, who knows? That is what makes them so frightening.) If not for Big Ugly, our colonel would like as not have been done for. Big Ugly dispatched both negroes with his bowie knife and then dragged our wounded Col. Cat to safety. Meanwhile, we widows were roused up. Poor, unfortunate darkies. They never stood a chance. They had knives, hammers and other tools in their grip—but we had Colt revolvers and shotguns in ours. Some surrendered without raising so much as an arm and dropped their weapons at their feet. Most, however, did not. We rounded them up and shot them.

And my Flora was among them. She was the hardest one for me to kill. But I must set the example. Other widows were watching. To have shown mercy would have meant condoning the revolt. And then where would that leave us? No, I marched right up to her and raised my revolver. I expected her to beg for her life. I still thought she was my Flora, don't you know. But she threw her shoulders back and looked me in the eye, as if to say, "I was never your Flora." Much as it pained me, I shot her dead.

Now I search for a safe place to grieve.

CUFF

WE'S A LONE passel of niggas now. The rest is dead. They like to kill Massa Cat, but he just laugh at his wounds, even while they stitch him up. Don't nobody tell me about the revolting. (I Col. Cat's nigga man.) Don't nobody tell me nothing, lest I tells Massa. But how you gonna git free without ever man they is? Ain't I a nigga? Think I won't bleed beside them, too? Think I had nothing to lose, too?

Doll and my baby is dead. I gots no wife. I gots no child. So what make them thinks I won't stand up and fight, too?

But don't nobody axed me. They thinks I still Massa Cat's nigga man. How can I be? When it was he what made my Dolly refugee with his Lorelei? To tend to his baby when she had a baby, too? And now they all dead. And who fault is it but Massa's? Ain't I a nigga?

Wish I was dead with the rest of them. I tried to run once. But I was monstrous dumb then.

Mebbe I still too dumb.

ELISHA TOOKE

DARKISH LLEWELLYN WARNED us the niggras would revolt. She said, "The rocks cried out," but I wouldn't listen to her. The last time she told me bout them rocks, I got raped. I didn't want to hear anymore of Darkish's witchcraft. But now I see. When Darkish Llewellyn speaks, you got no choice but to listen.

Now she tells us Col. Cat will live. He will survive his wounds, despite their going deep. His wounds will make him more alert than he already is. That our conspiracy again him is doomed to failure.

The colonel calls a council of war in his dog tent. Just the widow captains this time. When I see that there are no men, I think to myself, "He knows." But when he drinks his bottle of *Vin Mariani* and speaks, we can all breathe a sigh of relief. Darkish Llewellyn has not told on us. Our conspiracy is still alive, if withering on the vine.

"My widows," he says. "My lovelies. Seems like ever time I try to decide this War the God of Battles sticks his fucking beak into it. Last night we put down the last rebellion I shall tolerate in my camp. You dispatched your duty admirably. What's why I'm gonna reveal to you my plans. What's why you are all now captains of your own scouts."

"What does that mean?" I up and ask.

"It means, Capt. Tooke," he says. "you're chief of Tooke's Scouts."

He points to each widow and declares her a chief, too. Then he opens the ledger that has the names of Northrop's Scouts. He tears out a sheet for each of us to take. I read mine. They're all in Indiana.

"Indiana?" I cry. "We're already in Indiana! But Sherman is in Ohio!"

The others agree. Least they got assignments in Ohio. But we want Sherman. We don't care about no Northop's Scouts.

"So it's mutiny, then?" Cat says. I can still feel his body when it come up and under mine. It's like we think he plans to rape the whole lot of us.

"Not mutiny, sir," Brianna says. "We simply want to hit the heathen Sherman, first."

"It aggrieves me," Col. Cat says, "to think that you have come all this way only to buck against me now." He takes another swig of his "medicine" and says, "Cain't you bitches see I shall never die? That I am cursed to live? You wanted a hero. You wanted a Texas Ranger. Well, here I am. Now you question my authority. I ought to put all y'all on roots and whip your hides raw. But instead, I'm gonna channel that anger, that fury what I know's been bottled up ever since Tecumseh Sherman burnt your homes and did God knows what else to your bodies. All y'all are chiefs now. But if you want to burn Tecumseh Sherman's house down, then fine. He lives on East Main Street in Lancaster. His house is made of brick, just like your hard heads."

We suddenly grow outraged. "Brick?!" I say. "You didn't tell us that!"

"It matters not," he says. "Brick burns on the inside, just like a oven."

POLK INGRAHAM

She liked to stone the crows, I never had such loving. Darkish Llewellyn. Darkish Llewellyn. She's my mystery gal, my one true joy. Darkish Llewellyn. Darkish Llewellyn. Like her whole teeny body…

She come to me in the middle of the night ever since we crossed this side of the river into Yankeedom. I woen't lie. I felt scairt after the negroes revolted. I thought Uncle Calsas might been caught in the crossfire and was relieved to find him still alive. We're all lucky to still be alive, especially Cousin Cat.

She come to me that very night with tears in her eyes. "I tried to warn them," she said. I thought she meant us. But then she said, "I tried to warn them. But they wanted the freedom worse than their lives." Then she buried her head in this place in my shoulder I didn't know existed before she touched it and sobbed. We hadn't kissed each other since Mammoth Cave. So I lifted her chin and stole another kiss.

"The whole blamed world is gone to Halifax," I told her. "But leastways we have each other."

Darkish nestled into my shoulder, like a child. I pledged to protect her from all the world's sorrows with my heart. But she said, "You cain't protect me from him. I see that now."

"Who?!" I said, though I knew she meant Cat.

"Just hold me," she said. "Hold me aspell."

So I did. I commenced talking to her like I never talked to a gal before. Most of all I told Darkish about the Ingraham-Harvey feud. How I might could be destined to kill a Harvey, even Cat.

But Darkish told me, "The rocks tell me the feud ain't over. I ask them if you'll live, but that's all they told."

"I don't believe in rocks," I said.

"What do you believe in?" she asked.

I raised her chin again and said, "I believe in this." And I kissed her again. Darkish Llewellyn. Darkish Llewellyn. Liked to stone the crows.

ELIZA REED

WE CROSS INTO Ohio with nothing but our knives, guns, and a torn page from a ledger. I did not want to be made chief. I did not want this scout. But the colonel gave his orders. I do not have enough power alone to fight him. He is the father of my unborn baby, after all. The widows have taken to calling Cat Harvey *El Jefe del Jefes*. Chief of chiefs. It smacks of blasphemy. No one calls him "Gen. Cat." No one calls him "Galveston."

I read the list of names and towns from the torn page of the ledger. Our first town is Eldorado, where the names Sgt. Marcus McCleary, Pvts. Abraham Tolliver and James Isaacson reside. "We shall burn their homes by nightfall," I tell my widows. And they let out a chilling Rebel yell. My lieutenants are worried over me, however. They know I am with child. They must know by now. Some of the Mountain girls pick herbs that they say will help, but it seems I am not a Mountain girl. The brew only makes my sickness worse. My only comfort is Salome. She remained loyal, even when the negroes revolted. She remained loyal.

I wonder how many other widows he's made pregnant without their permission.

When the captains were conspiring against Cat, I thought of my own guilt in the matter. Somehow, I must have still loved the monster in human shape. Even now, as I ride at the head of a column of one hundred widows, I dare say I love the man. Oh God. What is wrong with me, that I love Cat Harvey—that rapist, my captor?

I told him the night before we broke apart. I mustered up enough strength to march into his dog tent without being summoned. I didn't stand on formalities. I addressed simply as "Cat."

"Miss Eliza," he replied. He still nursed his wounds from the revolt.

"Cat," I said, "I am with child. Your child."

He rested his left index finger beneath his nose, as if to smell it, while he considered my words, then said, "Do git out."

"I will not," I said. "I am with child. *Your* child. And I am here to declare that I intend to abort it." I hardly got the words out of my mouth before I knew they were indeed true. I could never, ever, bring Cat Harvey's child into the world. I could never, ever, let another being try and love the man.

"Eliza," he said, coolly. "I am a child of the Warchild. You think you can just abort my offspring like that? Tch. I think not. The God of Battles seen fit to blot out my family when he kilt my wife and daughter. But He also too give me hunnerds of widows who shall bear me children. What makes you think you're so special?"

When he stepped forward I drew my revolver and cocked it. "You'll not rape me again," I said.

He turned his head counterclockwise while reading my eyes, then said, "I often wondered if it were you what would kill me. So this is the end."

But I didn't ride all this way from Georgia country just to turn around and kill Cat Harvey, the very man who galvanized us widows in the first place.

"Go on, Eliza," he said to me. "Do it. King of the Mountain. You'll be the next *Jefe*. And what a fine one you'll be. I made a man of you. Go on, finish the job."

But I am not a man. I am a woman. That is more precious to me than burning a hundred homes. I felt the baby kick for the first time. It changed my heart. I holstered my revolver and turned-about. I imagine I must have wept.

But there are no more tears on the march. We ride into Eldorado not unlike desperados. There is still some bunting on the scanty buildings in celebration of Independence Day.

"Widows!" I shout. "Independence Day is *over*!"

They let loose another Rebel yell. We ride through the village in search of Northrop's Scouts.

I chose him.

LOT SHEPARD

It FEELS GOOD to be back in Montgomery County after such a long war. We taught those Rebels a lesson and a right smart one, too, but now is the season of peace. My only regret is that I never made commissioned officer before the War ended. Capt. Northrop never promised us commissions when we rode with him, but why else ride? Yes, we taught those Rebels a right smart lesson, but now I take my cues from Uncle Billy and look forward to a long and lasting peace. My wife, Emma, has already given me three healthy boys. I'd very much like to give her a girl.

I must admit that the War has left me restless. I crave the strenuous life now, whereas before I was something of a loafer. Was a time when Emma would make a list of things for me to do. I would grumble some (she says I'm an awful grumbler) but then I would go about my chores. But now I am the one giving myself chores. I awaken every morning restless and ready to exert myself in some fashion on the house and yard. It is a modest house we have. Nothing like the hulking plantation homes we burned in Georgia and all through the Carolinas. But I'm house-proud, you could say. You could say the War gave me a new perspective on protecting what's yours.

But each morning I also awaken with this sense that I am running out of time. That I won't have enough time to finish all of these projects I assign myself, despite the fact that I am still a young man with plenty of vim and vigor to last. Emma thinks I need religion. But I got plenty of that when I was a boy. In fact, I often joke with her, saying, "Don't look back too long, lest you turn into a pillar of salt." But she finds such jokes unfunny.

This morning I awakened with that same feeling, like the sands in the hour glass were somehow passing through a sieve. I skipped breakfast and got straight to work. There are pickets that need repainting and they won't repaint themselves.

I am halfway done with the job when I spot a sight I had not seen since the War. A little drummer boy dressed in butternut, no older than a cadet.

How strange! How peculiar! I instantly grew worried for the boy. After all, there are some hard feelings against the Rebels in Montgomery County. A boy dressed like that, no matter how old, might provoke some of the older boys to beat him up badly.

"You, boy!" I say. "Come here!"

I am about to scold him for wearing that uniform when he up and asks, "Can you tell me where I might could find Lot Shepard?"

How strange! How peculiar! I say, amused, "I am he."

The little Rebel takes his drumsticks and proceeds to beat out a Highland March in 7/8 time.

"See here, son," I say. "You're making a racket." But he does not cease. I have half a mind to jump my white picket fence and give him an old-fashioned spanking. Yet before I speak in my stern voice, I spot in the distance a miragey column of cavalry riding up the street. Though it is not night, they bear torches. Though I soon realize that these riders are women, I also see they are dressed as widows. "See here, son!" I bark at the little drummer boy. "Enough!"

And he stops.

That's when I hear the infernal Rebel yell, like a panther scream, let loose from the column of widows.

VELLA MORTON

I AM THE LAST captain Cat Harvey has raped. I could kill him, liked to haul off and *kill* him. It happened in the wee hours of the morning before I lit out on the march. Darkish Llewellyn had said I would be next, that the rocks "cried out" and told her so. And for the first time on this campaign I listened to the crazy gal. I stayed up nights waiting for an attack that never came. Always on my guard around the colonel, even after he made me chief of my own scouts. But I kept my guard up or stayed awake too long or something I don't know how. But when he ambushed me I found I hadn't the strength to even cry out, much less pummel the man. Liked to haul off and kill him. Liked to haul off and kill him dead.

He took my second virginity away, the virginity I was going to give Miss Bee. He took it. And I let him take it.

Now I have a Northrop Scout begging me for mercy. Sgt. Oliver Davis. We done burnt his home already. We made him watch it burn. It still smolders and there is fire we can still see. I tell him, "I am the Widow Morton! I am the Angel of Retribution! On your knees and admit your crimes!"

The sorry excuse for a coward Yankee does. Oliver Davis commences to tell me all the crimes he *didn't* commit: when Northrop's Scouts raided this town or that one, he didn't do this to that poor old woman or that to that poor young'un. He only followed orders, is what Oliver Davis says.

I show him my torn piece of paper from the ledger. "That your signature?" I say.

He don't answer but bursts into tears. Sorry coward. I could kill him, I could haul off and kill him. Instead, I wait to see what the widows wish to do. "Kill him!" some cry. "Throw him in the ash-heap and kill him!" "Burn him!" "Hang him!" "No, burn him!"

But then Miss Bee steps forward. All my widows know to shut up when Bee speaks. I listen to her with all my aching heart.

"Vella," she says. "Make a steer out of this rascal. Make believe it's Cat."

Oliver Davis screams for mercy now. It takes three of my widows to hold him down. I draw out my bowie knife while they shuck off his pants. Wish it was the colonel's balls I was cropping, instead of this pathetic excuse for a Yankee. But he'll do, awright. This rascal, he shall do.

I chose him.

ETHAN BRIARSTONE

I HAVE BEEN A "guest" of my captor for several weeks now, and Cat Harvey is on the warpath. He drinks bottles of *Vin Mariani* in our presence, his "medicine," which makes him more aggressive than he already is. It is the coca, I have decided. No wine makes a man so alert.

"Wordsworth," he tells me when we reach Franklin. "Come and git your word's worth." We are but a hundred miles from Gen. Sherman's home in Lancaster. I keep waiting for our soldiers, state militia, home guards—*someone*—to stop this madness and release me from my captivity, but it seems that I remain in Cat Harvey's orbit for now. So I oblige him, my captor.

Nothing surprises me anymore, not even the fact that Cat Harvey appears like a circus freak among circus freaks in his black dress and clown makeup.

"Mr. Ethan," he calls me. The second time he has used my proper name. "The Eunuch-tarian."

We have had several discussions about my Unitarian faith. Each one more dangerous than the next. So I prepare to meet my Maker because I shall not have my faith mocked.

"Why do you persist mocking that which you clearly don't understand?" I say. "Am I to live or die?"

"I have not yet decided, Mr. Ethan," he says.

"Then you have not given the matter much consideration."

"Ha," he says. "You Yankees. Always talking yourselves into a corner."

"I would rather use words than fists," I say. "I would rather die for something I said that was right than live with something I did that I knew was wrong."

"Mmm," he grunts. "You still think I'm capable of redemption."

"No man is beyond redemption," I declare.

Cat Harvey folds his hands in the attitude of prayer. He does not speak for a long moment, then says, "When I seen Christ burn on the cross in that Georgia cornfield, with the crows hovering above the smoke, I knew I were not one of his apostles. I knew that cause Jesus were never a man of honor. He *let* the Romans take him. He *let* them crucify him. Then he watched and *let* the South fall to pieces like so much overcooked meat dripping off the bone. I knew I warn't his apostle. I were the Roman soldier what stabbed him in the side."

"I don't believe any of what you say," I tell him, then brace myself for an attack.

"What do you care, Unitarian?" he retorts. "Probably believe in Mohammed, like a fucking Muslimman, don'cha?"

"What I believe is that you can stop all of this. You have the power to make it stop. It's not too late."

"Oh, but it is," he says. "I have made my peace with my fate. I'm damned. And so is Tecumseh Sherman. He's gonna reap what he sowed, just like the rest of us in this sorry world."

"And then what?" I say. "What next?"

I can see that he has not yet considered this.

Finally, he replies, "What next don't matter much in 1865."

METTA DAHLGREN

W<small>E RIDE A</small> circuit round Springfield, just as Jeb Stuart had rode round McClellan. I want the town to know that my ladies have arrived. None of my girls ride side-saddle anymore. We come bearing torches, but we are just as precise as the villain Sherman. We shall only set fire to the vile homes of Northrop's vile Scouts. A signal fire for vile Sherman to see all the way in Lancaster.

So many of my girls wish to ride straight to Lancaster. But now I see the poetry in Cat Harvey's strategy. He wants his widows champing at the bit. Lancaster is the salient of this campaign. For Gen. Sherman, there shall be no mercy nor escape.

The first house we burn belongs to a corporal, Abner Applewood. We are vexed because we find him not at home, the coward. But at least his wife and two daughters get to see their beautiful home go up in flames, just as mine had not three months ago.

"Tell your man," I shout down from my Princess Ann, "we shall return for him!"

The crying woman picks up the nearest rock to throw at me, but one of my widows shoots her in the hand. The woman's daughters scream. It is a sound that is dear to my ears.

When Cat Harvey raped me, when our *Jefe del Jefes* raped my body, he planted a seed of hate that has swelled like Eliza Reed's pregnant belly. All is not forgiven, not even once we burn Sherman's home to ashes. I shall never forgive Cat Harvey for the brutal way he treated me, indeed for the brutality he showed us all. How many of my widows has he raped? How many have come to me, shamefaced and pregnant? No, *El Jefe* must die. Then we can memorialize him. We shall teach our children that he was a hero. Children need heroes, especially hero-fathers. Cat Harvey shall be more use to our Cause dead than alive.

A lady needs a man in 1865 like a hawk needs a hot air balloon.

I chose him.

JAKE LIBERTY

W<small>HEN THE BUGLE</small> blowed for us to mount up, I thought, "This must be another drill." Here I signed up for Mr. Lincoln's army, a free man, and all they give me is guard duty the whole War. I wanted to fight, and even die if I had to, for my country. I want to free other slaves, the way I been freed. Instead, I been on shovel detail. I must of dug some two thousand graves burying Rebel prisoners at Camp Chase. Missed the whole War.

Yet once we mounted up our hosses, the captain, he tells us, "All right, you niggers, now it's time to show your mettle."

I growed to despise our captain. He hates us the way the overseer hated us, especially when he drinks. He give us our last names. I wanted to name myself Jake Liberty. But he give me MacDonald instead.

My real name is Jake Liberty, soon as I get out of this here cavalry.

I want to ax him, "Where all we riding, captain?" But that gets you a swat from his rider's crop. So we all must wait till we ride southwest out of Columbus. It is hot and July.

"Damn bitch women," he says over and over again. None of us know what he means until we reach a meadow where we find a whole heap of armed widows taken by surprise. They mount their horses and mules as soon as they spot us. "Charge them, you fools!" our captain yells. "Charge!"

We have been trained for this day. We don't think. We act. Our captain is a no-account drunk of a nigga-hater, but he leads the charge. I give him that much. I give him that.

It all happens so fast. We pitch into them and turn them every which way but loose. They shoot at us, we shoot at them. I just shoot to stay alive. Never thought I'd come to see the day when I would shoot a white lady, much less a white widow, but I'll shoot one that trying to shoot me. I'll shoot her dead.

It is a rout. Some widows flee, but most fight to the death like wild Indians. But we are the 12th U.S. Colored Troops. We shall not be moved, not when we come this far. The blue gunsmoke smells of rotten eggs. I hope I never have to smell it again.

There is a widow that coughs up blood, but is still breathing. Our captain dismounts and strides over to her to shoot her point blank. God as my witness, I don't remember raising my revolver, but I shoot the captain in the back of his head.

Nobody breathes, except for the widow.

I quickly dismount and run over to help the widow raise up. She reaches for her shotgun, but I kick it out of the way. I expect any second for one of the other niggas to open fire, but they don't. I don't even have to tell them that it was justice, what I did.

I cradle the poor widow in my arms as she coughs more blood. "Go on and say your last, honey," I say to her.

"Tell Darkish…" she says, but first she must swallow more blood. "Tell her that Elisha Tooke says, 'She was right.'"

Then Elisha Tooke dies in my arms.

JOHN HENRY HOLIDAY

We HEAR ABOUT the massacre at Mount Sterling from all sources. "Rumors," *El Jefe* says. Cat Harvey has run out of *Vin Mariani* and needs some more medicine. But when some widows who survived the battle return, they confirm our worst fears. Capt. Elisha Tooke and all her widows, dead. Capts. Dahlgren and the Morton sisters, dead. Jincy McBride and her Mountain troopers, all dead except for Jincy, who must of fled the field. Capts. O'Quinn and Reed, somewhere out there missing. All killed by nigger troopers who fought like the Devil, and we are now in their pursuit.

I count two dozen widows, a passel of Texas Rangers and three niggers left. We are defeated, just like the Confederacy itself.

The widows want blood, Cat Harvey's blood. But they have yet to strike. I won't be there to see it, neither. I throw into my tricks the only things I know of value in this world: the Colt revolver I got from Cat Harvey and a deck of cards I got from his brother. Doc Holiday will survive.

METTA DAHLGREN

Reports of my death are a calumny against my good name. I should say I am recovering from my wounds rather nicely, considering I am left for dead.

I had awakened after the battle without my guns in a strange bed in a strange hovel with all sorts of smelly herbs draped from its ceiling. It was dusk-dark. I wanted to scream. I dared not scream.

"Awake then?" the voice of an old crone spoke from the darkness. She struck a match and its flame illumined her prunish face and long, wild gray hair.

"Are you a witch?" I was afraid to ask. Instead, I asked, "Who are you?"

"This is *my* cabin," the old crone said as she lit her candles. I could not tell by her accent if she were Southern or Northern. "I should be asking you the same question."

"I am Metta Dahlgren of the Georgia Dahlgrens," I openly declared.

"Oh, Your Highness," the crone said, then chuckled to herself. "You'uns a long way from home."

"Where am I?" I said. The last thing I remembered was calling for Princess Ann, my dead warhorse, on the battlefield.

"You'uns is safe in the forest," she replied. "Won't nobody shoot you here."

"Am I your prisoner?" I said.

"Drink," said the crone as she handed me a dipper containing a strange smelling liquid. It was awful and I said so. The crone didn't seem to care. She insisted I drink again and much to my distaste I obliged her.

"You have not answered my questions," I told her. "Who are you? Where am I? Am I your prisoner?"

"Tut-tut, Your Highness," she said. "Let's see to those wounds first."

I resisted her aid, but it proved too futile and exhausting. I had lost a lot of blood, I discovered, and I was riddled with bullet holes. I wanted to go home. I wanted my Mama. When I saw my own blood seep out of one wound while the crone applied her poultice, I suppose I must have fainted.

Now I have awakened to dawn's early twilight. The crone holds a bundle of herbs and she is rubbing them all over her hovel. It looks like witchcraft.

"What are you doing?" I ask.

"Smudging," she says.

"What is *smudging*?"

She turns to me and says, "You brought lots of bad spirits with you. Hate. Sorrow. Revenge. Who is Cat?"

"Cat?" I say. I take a moment, then say, "He was once my champion."

"Knight in shiny armor, eh?" the crone says, as she resumes smudging the entire hovel. "I had one of those when I was your age. Always shiny, their armor."

"What else did I say?" I am not known for talking in my sleep.

"It is time for you to rest, Your Highness."

I must have passed out instantly because when I awaken I am alone with my memories and it is dusk once again. "Ma'am?" I call out. "Ma'am?" But she has not returned home. If I could just rise, I could make my escape. But I am too weak and weary, my wounds too great. Perhaps this witch has cast her spell on me and I do not wish to leave. Where shall you go, Metta Dahlgren, once you recover, if you recover, where shall you go?

I think now about Cat Harvey. How wrong I was to follow such a man. I chose him, but why? What is it in a woman that makes her give up her power so freely to such men as these? At what cost do we cling to the fantasy of the beau ideal? All through the War we looked to men as our saviors— Lee, Johnston, Hood—we even prayed to Jesus as if he were a man of honor. We starved for Jeff Davis and watched our homes burn under the deliberate watch of Gen. Sherman. Men start the wars, like little boys on a fairground, so it is up to the women to finish them. I took up arms, thinking I would follow a boy soldier to victory. I took up arms. What was I expected to do? I took up arms, hoping to find my revenge in the saddle when I learned the ways of the gun. I took up arms. I killed Flora, the only maid-servant I have ever known. Now she is dead, and God knows all she wanted was a taste of freedom. I took up arms and yet those arms did not defend me against Cat Harvey when he raped my body. Is it wrong to love your rapist when you are left with so little else in the world? Every night I dream I am pregnant with Cat Harvey's child, a Rebel girl; and every morning I pray to the cold angels in Heaven that this is not true.

You are no longer a victim, Metta Dahlgren, you have blood on your hands. I no longer care whether or not Sherman lives, whether or not his home burns; I only care about living long enough to see my way home, though all that remains of it is a brick chimney rising like a sentinel. I want to live long enough to see Mother again. She will be ashamed when she learns of my adventures. "Ladies don't..." is Mother's favorite expression. But Mother, if I am a poetess then I am a warrior-poet.

And I am not a ladylike poet.

BRIANNA O'QUINN

Aʟʟ ᴍʏ Sʜᴇʟɪᴀs and Shannons are dead. I didn'a ask for this life, you know. I didn'a ask to be made a woman. Banshee O'Quinn they once called me. To be sure, I give the Rebel yell like a banshee, but what is a throaty yell against men that dare demand they be free? To be sure, they had Spencers and Enfields while we had revolvers and knives. But that wasn'a the reason the Negroes licked us at Mount Sterling. They wanted stronger than revenge: the soul's urge to be free. So only now do you understand it, Banshee O'Quinn. Now, at the end, do ya?

I didn'a ask for this life, but I was made a woman all the same. Now I'm trapped in a bleeding Protestant church with an angry mob outside and nothing but the bullets in my revolvers to show for my journey. They want to clap me in irons, or worse, lynch me. But I'll not give them the satisfaction. I'm on my bleeding period.

Cat Harvey, you eight stone bastard. You raped my gob and I let you live. Why? I chose him, but why? Did I need a chieftain so bad that I had to follow the first man that showed a stiff prick at the world? Am I not a Celtic girl? Did we not have warrior women in the old country? Did we not have heroines in Ireland? Yet ours was a sisterhood of hate. 'Tis why it has all come to this.

I shall never see Ireland now. The only Dublin I have seen is in my native state of Georgia.

"Come on out, girl, you're surrounded!" one of the heathen Yankees shouts to me.

"Ask me bollocks!" I cry. "My name is Banshee O'Quinn!" I announce, for all the world to feel. "I'll not come out till I'm good and ready!"

I would say such things even if I wasn'a on my bleeding period. But the flux makes me particularly surly.

All my fine Shelias and Shannons are dead. The widows' brigade passes into myth. They want Banshee O'Quinn, then I'll give it them! I take off my widow's weeds and smear menstrual blood on my face. I resolve to step out of this Protestant church, naked as the day I was born, show my red Irish gee to them all with six-guns firing! *I am Banshee O'Quinn! I am Boudicca!*

ELIZA REED

So MANY WIDOWS...so many pregnant widows dead. I would have been among them, too, had I not broken free before the battle and fled the scene. Darkish Llewellyn was right. She is always right. She said we would die before reaching Gen. Sherman's home, that we would die before we could even look upon, much less burn it, and she was right. Why did I flee the battle, like a perfect coward? Because I had a baby to protect, even if it is Cat Harvey's.

I ride alone. Salome abandoned me before the battle even commenced. She saw her chance for freedom, and she took it. Instead of getting sad or shocked, like I am want to do, I stood out there alone for the first time in my life and realized that if I proceed to give battle, I shall surely die. And then what would happen to the baby growing inside me? So how can I blame Salome for taking to freedom? Isn't that what I have done myself?

It is a lonely road back home. I am five hundred miles from nowhere. I am a stranger in Ohio, just as I shall be a stranger in Kentucky and Tennessee. My only fear? That Cat Harvey will learn I am still alive and pursue me. That he will find me and catch me. And do I have the courage to shoot him? Do I have a mother's courage to defeat him?

Why did I ever fall in love with that beast? I was not so young and foolish. I was not a virginal maiden when we first met. I was a war widow, after all. What is my love for him now but the piece of science that makes the clock click and whir and sometimes chime?

I have made the decision to keep my child. I shall not kill myself or it.

We both shall live. It would be easier on us if we didn't, God knows. But if I am to face 1865 alone, then it is a comfort to know we face it alone together.

Rumors abound. I hear about him everywhere. That they have captured Cat Harvey, "Galveston, the Rodeo Clown," and have taken him to Camp Chase where he shall surely hang for his crimes. That they have lynched Cat Harvey on the nearest sour apple tree. Or that Cat Harvey is still alive. Rumors abound. A posse seems to form in every town I pass through, which looks askance at me, a lone widow on her horse. I know I should hope for his death. It would be safer for me, for us, if Cat Harvey were dead. But we have a soul-tie, he and I. Albeit one consummated by rape. I somehow know that not only is he alive: Cat Harvey is still at large. It saddens me to think that he might yet try and fight Sherman. Like a boy trying to fight off the ocean. And then what shall become of my baby's father?

I know I should shun all memory of him, but I can't. He was once my one true love. My hero in a gray shell coat with butternut patches. I know he lives with his afflictions and shall run out of medicine, if indeed he hasn't already. I wish I could somehow comfort Cat in a cage. I wish I could put my arms around him as I press up against the bars.

BEE BREWSTER

I RETURNED FROM THE battlefield prepared to kill him. To once and for all kill him. All the Milledgeville widows are dead because of Cat Harvey, *El Jefe del Jefes*. It is all because of *him*. How many of us did he rape, besides me? How many of us did he impregnate with his awful seed? I know I am carrying his baby and shall have to opium it to death. It could very well kill me, but I shall not bring Cat Harvey's child into the world. I shall not be reminded of that rape that happened in my own house. I shall never look at another pair of Cat Harvey's green eyes.

But worst of all, he killed Vella. Not with his own gun. He killed her with his outrageous dream of glorious revenge against Gen. Sherman. We burned whole blocks of houses smoking out Northrop's Scouts, knowing that word would get back to Sherman. Would Vella have lived, would we all have yet lived, had we simply gone after Sherman in the first place? Or would we have yet lived had we never left burnt Georgia at all? We would all still be in Milledgeville, my sisters, if it weren't for Cat Harvey.

But then I would never have met Vella. I would have passed her on the street, probably, and never said a word to her. It is hard for me to explain my love for her. She was in love with me in that most unnatural way I didn't know a woman could love. I kissed Vella but she kissed me back. I held Vella but she held me back. She undid so much of the damage that Cat Harvey had wrought, all with her two gentle hands. She kissed me here and here and there. How I wished that it would somehow awaken reciprocal feelings in me. Vella deserved better. But her lips, her tongue and her hands could only undo what had already been done; they could not *do*. Vella deserved better. She always called me "Miss Bee," despite my protests that she simply call me "Bee." The only time she said this was on the battlefield when she saved my life at the cost to her own.

Why did I not kill Cat Harvey? Because when what widows we had left ganged up on him, I saw that he was hurting. He had run out of his "medicine" and cast about looking for more. He tried to rally us to raid Columbus, where there would be a druggist; this we knew. He was a pathetic specimen of manhood. He was weak. He looked at us two dozen widows as if we were hungry wolves circling their prey. Maybe we were. Why did I not kill Cat Harvey? Why did I, in fact, save his life? Because killing was too good for him? No. I saved his life because I knew that that would save *mine*.

I spoke up just before the widows could kill him. "Wait!" I cried. Some of the widows wanted to ignore me, proceed with the killing. But I jumped into the circle and protected Cat with all the ferocity his own mother would have shown him. I found my power that day. All the widows recognized it, too. "We shall banish him!" I decreed.

"Like hell!" one widow yelled and tried to squeeze off a round, but another widow raised her arm. They would not kill one of their kind to get to Cat.

"We shall banish him!" I decreed. "Banish him!" Then I turned to Cat Harvey, my rapist, and said, "Step out of our circle, Cat Harvey. Step out of it forever."

He was so slight. Full of his cravings and afflictions. He had not the strength to protest. He merely slunked off, like a lone wolf banished from the pack. None of the widows fired another shot.

"But Bee," a widow said. "He raped us."

"Killing him won't unrape you," I said then stepped out of the widows' circle, too.

Now I am the new leader. *El Jefe del Jefes*. And I have but one order: we are heading home. Some to Kentucky, others to Tennessee, most to Georgia with me.

I only wish Vella were coming with me.

JINCY MCBRIDE

W<small>HEN</small> I <small>CATCHED</small> up to the other widows on the road to Kentucky, I seen that Cat Harvey was not with them. I learned they banished him. "Banish?" I said. "Which way did you banish him?" They thought I liked to kill him, just like I knowed some of the others would. But they was wrong.

"Come with us," Bee Brewster said.

And I said, "No."

"He can't hurt you anymore," she said.

Those words cut me deep. But I was stern and resolved. It been two moons since I had the flux. I knowed I was carrying Cat Harvey's young'un in my belly. No way I was bout to let the critter come into the world without setting eyes upon his daddy neither. I chose him. Why, I reckon I'll never know. Maybe I'm cursed, like as not. I got the curse of Cat Harvey and cain't git it off'n me.

The band of widows Bee Brewster leads goes one way, but I go the other. If Cat Harvey is banished, then it looks like I am too. We'll be a banished family, one way or the other.

UNCLE CALSAS

M R. C AT NEVER come back with his widows, so we menfolk search for him. But we find no hide nor hair of any of them. They gone. What all we find on the roadside though was a widow's dress with clown makeup wiped on it. We all knows it Mr. Cat's then. All us gits quiet. Then the white-folks looks to me for what all to do, for where all to go.

Now I seen everthing. They tell me it 1865, but it Year Zero as far as ole Calsas is concerned when they look to an old nigga like me for a leader. I knows how it come erbout. Mr. Wyatt ain't been the same since the widows hung his twin. He keeps rubbing his arm, as if it was missing, the way Mr. Gibby do. Mr. Worth, he all for lighting out for Chicago. I knows this without his saying so. His revenge is there waiting for him in Chicago. But Mr. Smit'll have the shakes and the goes if he don't git some corn liquor in him—and quick. Meanwhile, Polk aims to marry that Darkish gal. And Big Ugly and Rainy is lost as they can be without Mr. Cat to tell them what all to do. So that leave me.

I wants to go home. I wants to see my Serena and our cheerdren and grandbabies. I wants us to take our Freedom in Texas. Together, as man and wife oughts to do. I been away from Serena going on four years. I left playing my mandoline, now I play the blues.

So I say, "We might could go back to Texas...?"

CLAYTON CHADWICK

I RUN A CLEAN newspaper at the *Ohio State Journal*. There are some standards more important than "the truth." When the War was on, I kept to the standards of decency and good taste while my competitors ran all sorts of muckety-do in their rags. (Imagine, placing sketches of the dead on the front page!) No, I print only the clean truth, or it does not go into my newspaper.

So, no, I did not print the outrageous Battle of Mount Sterling that occurred mere days ago in my newspaper. Wild stories pouring into Columbus—widows with guns, Negroes on horseback, a clown named Galveston at large—enough! I run a clean and decent newspaper. I have no tolerance for such muckety-do. Let the rags print that, that *sensationalism* that's all the rage these days. I speak for the Public Mind, not the public. Our best citizens would tar and feather me if I were to print such a disgraceful, ridiculous tale.

So why my son-in-law (my daughter, Meg, insisted I hire him) brought in this Ethan Briarstone from the *New York Herald*, I shall never know. It seems Meg married him just to vex me. I met with the man. I dare not call him a journalist. I met Mr. Briarstone in my office, and boy did he spin a tale. He claimed to have been held captive by this Galveston, the Rodeo Clown. He knew his true name, too, which escapes me now. He could supply me with all sorts of details about these armed widows the public is talking about on the streets of Columbus. How he witnessed the Battle of Mount Sterling, where he made his escape, and that he could recount it for our paper. He only asks that we print the truth.

"The *truth*?" I said. "What do you intend to mean by the truth?"

"I only wish to get the story right," Mr. Ethan Briarstone said.

"And what about the *New York Herald*?" I said.

"They wish to print a story that is false," he said. "*The Herald* wants to use Galveston as a case for radical Reconstruction."

"Are you not a Union man?" I asked.

"I am."

"Yet you did not fight for your country," I said.

"No," he said. "I am Unitarian. I seek the truth."

"The truth!" I bellowed. "Confound it, man, do you hear yourself?" He was taken aback. But I felt myself boiling over with sheer fury. "We do not print the truth! We print the facts! Now out!"

My son-in-law showed him out. I am not a violent man, but I dare say I came close to losing my temper in my own office.

A Unitarian. Imagine!

ETHAN BRIARSTONE

And so I was shown the door.

I imagine I shall quit the business altogether. I have been a professional witness all my adult life. Perhaps it is time I take up another trade.

As I tramp through the streets of Columbus, exercising my newfound freedom, I cannot help but think that Cat Harvey is somewhere out there still at large. Would he kill me on the spot if he saw me? Does he even give a damn? I wish to write a pamphlet about my experience, perhaps even a book. But I wouldn't know how to write about my last encounter with Cat Harvey.

It was right before we reached the aptly named Yankeetown, not three miles south of Mount Sterling. He had run out of his medicine and grew agitated and cast about for relief.

"Where's Darkish?" he kept saying. He intended to rape her, I imagine, but thank God the strange girl had ridden off with the gold alone.

Although he was agitated, my captor was also sober, so I took this opportunity to reason with the manchild. I did not beg for my life. I did not demand he release me. I merely said, "It is not too late, Cat."

"There's that word again—*Redemption*," he said, as if I had indeed said it.

"You have the power to end this," I said. "Even if you succeed in killing Sherman and burning his house, what would it possibly profit?"

He stared into me with those lost eyes, which didn't look so bright anymore. It tested my faith in the power of redemption to look into those eyes.

How could I describe them in a pamphlet, much less a book? Words fail us most when we wish to give name to the mysteries of our existence.

Then Cat Harvey broke down and began to cry—only for a moment, then his awful rage reappeared. He drew his gun on me and once more I prepared to meet my Maker. Then he placed the barrel against his temple. How could I explain with words how I simultaneously held my breath and yelled, "Cat, no!"

But his revolver went *snick*.

Astonished, Cat checked the cylinder of his weapon: empty. He looked at me, as if I had something to do with it. Then he laughed without mirth. What words could I use to describe that laugh? He actually laughed.

"Darkish," he finally said, as if she were standing right there. "Oh, Darkish. You took my bullets. You wanted me to ride into battle without a bullet to my name."

I wanted to reason with him, but he was mad. We arrived at the battle just in time to watch it unfold in his cracked spyglass, to watch his widows' ranks get decimated, to watch the remainder of them retreat. He rode after these widows, and I saw my chance to escape. So I took it.

But now I wonder if such a man is indeed beyond redemption. It has rocked my faith to its foundation. Why would God build a man in order to tear him down so? Why have redemption at all, if not for someone so lost in the wilderness of his pain?

POLK INGRAHAM

WHERE IS SHE, where is my jewlarky, Darkish? What am I s'posed to do without her? How am I s'posed to live?

WILLIAM TECUMSEH SHERMAN

I CONFESS, WITHOUT SHAME, that I'm sick and tired of fighting. Its glory
is all moonshine. After the great triumph that we had in Washington, I grew
gloomy once again. Lincoln is dead, and I have been given command of the
Military Division of the Mississippi. Lincoln is dead, and I have dominion
over everything west of the Mississippi and east of the Rockies. I have hardly
had time to embrace Ellen and our brood. "I am to go West," I told her.
She didn't speak to me for two days.

Politicians whisper in my ear these days, hoping to ride my coattails.
"You could be president," they say. "President Sherman." I hate them as
much as I hate journalists who always ask of my affairs. I have no damn use
for the lot of them.

No, I wish to enjoy my time in Ohio while I can. Then light out for the
West, where the future of America lay. And yet I find myself in a terrible
gloom. Grant is the only one who understands me now, and he's still in
Washington, despite my warnings. Ellen says it's because of the baby we lost
while I marched through Georgia. "Now that you are home, you must
grieve," she says. But I do not wish to remember such things. I try and put
them out of my mind.

Instead, I must confess, I miss the South. I miss its lazy ways, its hospitality, before all this Secession madness got a hold of it. I warned the South.
I warned my Southern friends their beloved Southland would be drenched
in blood when I resigned my post at the Military Academy in Baton Rouge.

Now look what they made me do.

I sit on my front porch and nod at the passersby, men and women who once considered me crazy, and wait until it is time to head West.

Maybe I am crazy. Sometimes I want to burn my hometown down. News has reached me that some madman named Galveston has ridden into Ohio with a band of wild women, widows, I sometimes hear. Maybe I am crazy because I sit on my porch and hope to God some madman would just try and invade the sanctuary of my home.

We have war widows in Lancaster, too.

They pass by often. Sometimes they tell me of a husband or brother who had served under me. They cry; they always cry. I lie to them. I say, "Oh yes, I believe I remember him." Then I let them talk some more about their loved one and how he died.

On this particular day, as I sit on my porch and watch the yard, I see a strange young widow riding on muleback. Young widows are strange enough, but this one is so tiny I mistake her for a little girl. I sigh a deep sigh and expect for her to come talk to me when she halts her mule in front of my house. I rise from my seat to greet her when I spot her sidearms belted around her waist. It is only then that I realize she is, in fact, a woman.

"You there, Miss," I say. "What do you want?"

By the gods in Olympus, she does not say a word yet her silence speaks volumes. It says to me my life hangs in the balance of her decision. Should I move, she will draw and shoot. Should I not move, she might very well do the same. But she has not yet decided. Not since bloody Shiloh have I been so afraid.

I watch her as she turns in profile a moment, then look on in horror as she furrows her brow and points the finger of *Judgment* at me. She says not a word, but her silence seems to scream from the living rock I stand on: "*You!*"

It lasts only for a moment, but it feels like an eternity. When she stops pointing that tiny finger of hers, I release my breath. She stays on the mule and, without haste, rides away.

I march through my yard to my stone steps leading to the sidewalk, but

I dare not go any further. "You, there!" I yell. I'm livid, practically rabid. "I demand you come back here! Do you hear me?! I demand you come back!"

ACKNOWLEDGEMENTS

So many people encouraged me while I wrote this novel. I am profoundly grateful to *This Side of the River*'s early readers: Josh Chisom and Christopher Bundrick. I am also indebted to the following readers: Marty Kelly and Cait McFarland. My sincerest gratitude to Michael McFarland, Cynthia Shearer, Tom Franklin and Barry Hannah, my former creative writing instructors. I raise a glass of bourbon to all my writer and poet friends from Sewanee, Breadloaf and Oxford! More bourbon for my friends at Square Books and Burke's Books! My appreciation also extends to Texas Tech University's Southwest Collection's Library and the University of Texas's Barker Center, where I did most of my archival research for this novel. I am sincerely grateful to my editor and publisher, Neil White, who along with his awesome staff has brought this novel to market. I would also like to thank Julie Schoerke and her team at JKS Communications for getting the word out. I want to thank my family. They are all great storytellers. To my brother Matt and his family. To my mom, who taught me how to read. To my dad, who believed in this novel till the day he died. Lastly, I save my heartfelt gratitude for my loving wife, Lonette Robertson Stayton. You are not only a great writer, Nikki, you are great reader and this novel has clearly benefited from having your eyes on it.